THE FINAL NOTCH

Sheriff Massingham and Deputy Brack Bowman have had their lives ruined by the ruthless criminal element that preys on their fellows. They have both devoted much of their time to redressing the balance, but once again a killer strikes. Massingham and Bowman meet up, each with his own reason for hunting down this merciless murderer. Their partnership eventually leads to poetic justice for the killer, climaxing in a bloody battle.

KEN McKEOWN

THE FINAL NOTCH

Complete and Unabridged

LINFORD
Leicester

First published in Great Britain in 1993 by
Robert Hale Limited
London

First Linford Edition
published 1996
by arrangement with
Robert Hale Limited
London

British Library CIP Data

McKeown, Ken,
The final notch.—Large print ed.—
Linford western library
1. English fiction—20th century
I. Title
823.9'14 [F]

ISBN 0-7089-7885-1

Published by
F. A. Thorpe (Publishing) Ltd.
Anstey, Leicestershire

Set by Words & Graphics Ltd.
Anstey, Leicestershire
Printed and bound in Great Britain by
T. J. Press (Padstow) Ltd., Padstow, Cornwall

This book is printed on acid-free paper

For my daughter Barbara, and for my nieces Caroline, Jackie and Angela, with all my love.

Once again the author would like to thank Nick Berry, for coping with a horrendous draft to type the work. Relax Nick . . . I'm struggling to learn how to use a Word Processor!

1

THE trapper watched the burly man approach; he'd spotted him way off, where the horizon danced in a heat haze.

He carefully laid a pelt over his old .60 Hawken rifle before the man was close enough to see it. The trapper's keen old eyes noted the hawk-like features and downturned mouth. No sense in taking chances. The man exuded trouble; a mean cuss straddling a palomino that was thin, nervy, and plain tuckered.

The man pulled up with a savage jerk. Not a horse lover.

"Chaw sure smells good, friend," he grated.

With a wave of his left hand the trapper invited the stranger to join him. His right hand stayed close to the pelt.

"Ain't much, mister. But you're welcome, and the cawfee ain't at all bad," he replied.

Hunkered by the fire, the burly man tore at the venison as if he had a personal score to settle with the meat.

His suit had once been well cut and expensive; but a city suit takes a hammering on a long ride. The man was dusty and dishevelled and, to the trapper's trained nose the sweat stains were more than just visible.

"Bin trappin' round here long?" he asked, shooting a keen glance at the old man. "Don't seem much round here."

His big hands ripped another lump of venison. Thick fingers poked it greedily down his throat.

"Nope, you're right, mister. I was workin' the territory over the other side o' Lewis. Then 'bout a dozen mean lookin' characters come from nowheres. I upped an' pulled out. Dropped into Lewis; now I'm headed south."

The big man leaned forward. His

2

voice was a shade too casual.

"Much ahappenin' there? How did y'find things, friend?"

The trapper gulped hot coffee and wiped his mouth. "Lewis? Just like any other ant-hill; folk rushin' about an' bumpin' each other's asses!"

He spat into the fire and watched it sizzle on a flaking branch. "Big funeral just afore I left. Seems the judge's daughter died givin' birth. Husband had just bin swore in as a depity that very day. They was a popular couple, name of, er, Bowman. The way folk was goin' on you'd a thought no one ever died in that town!" He raked horny fingers through his hair. "Think it was Bowman. Yeah, Bowman."

The knuckles gripping the tin mug opposite him gleamed bone white. "This feller Bowman. Son-in-law to the judge, an' a depity y'say? Doin' all right for hisself, worn't he? Wives an' brats are overrated luxuries, to my way o' thinkin', an' pretty gals are three to the dollar, eh?"

3

The trapper shook his grizzled head, trying to recall what he had heard. "Seems gals wouldn't be on his mind. Got other fish to fry. About three year ago a feller lit outa Lewis just one jump ahead o' Bowman. They say the jasper was a back-shootin' sonofabitch who'd framed an' killed Bowman's father. Then scooted outa town as if his ass was on fire when he heard the son was around. Tough hombre, that Bowman." The old man hawked another stream into the flames. "Anyways, where's yuh headed, mister?"

The dark-suited stranger ignored the question while he dug a half-smoked cheroot from his vest pocket. Lighting it, he inhaled deeply, then trickled out smoke.

"Where am I headin'?" he breathed to himself. "Not for Lewis, that's for sure. Not yet awhiles."

He turned red-rimmed eyes on the trapper.

"Where'm I headin'? If it's any business o' your'n, I'm headin' for

Massingham Town. Know it, friend?"

"Can't say's I do, but it's a fair ride west o' here."

The other man's eyes burned into him, and he shivered.

"Lissen, old-timer, there was a young sheriff in that town, an' they named it after him! He still there, or has someone put a bullet in him, eh?"

"Nope, he's still there, mister. They say he's got that town so peaceful folk call it Sleepy Valley!"

As he recalled the gossip he'd heard in saloons all over the country, he grinned at the burly man.

"He's said to be lightnin' on the draw, but he don't need to draw these days. They got a fence round the darned town an' a gatehouse where guns have to be handed in! But there's a hell of a lotta fist fightin' goin' on, an' young Massingham punches with the best of 'em. Undertaker's real poor, they say."

When the big man stood, his voice was casual once more. The trapper's

5

hair stirred and tingled at the roots; he'd been in some tight spots in his time, but never one that felt as bad as this. A sensation of helplessness, of chill inertia, crept over him. The big man pointed at him.

"So yuh reckon this Bowman guy's lookin' for Frankie Dorrell?"

The trapper shrugged. "That's what they said in Lewis. Wonder where the jasper . . . "

His blood ran cold and his voice came out as a hoarse whisper. "Wait a minute, mister. I never said his name was Dorrell. How'd you know that?"

Lips pulled back in a stiff grin, he inched his hand under the pelt. How he wished he packed a handgun, and not just that heavy old Hawken rifle.

The stranger's laugh was as friendly as water gurgling down a drain.

"Dorrell's bin a long ways from here, Santa Fe in fact. Now he's on his way to Massingham. Visit an ole pal an' rob the bank before goin' to Lewis to take care o' that Bowman feller."

"Rob the Massingham bank? He must be somethin' special," the trapper observed. "Me, I'd sooner wrestle a she-bear for her cub!"

There was an ugly gleam in the stranger's eyes. "Dorrell *is* somethin' special, an' you better not forget it."

Cold sweat filmed the trapper's brow, his arms and legs, and pasted his shirt to his back as his hand crept nearer the Hawken. His fingers touched the smooth wood of the butt and felt along to the trigger. All he had to do was lift the gun with one hand and whip the pelt away with the other. The big gun had felled many a buffalo at a mile and stopped grizzly bears in their tracks. Could it save him now?

Again he attempted a smile, trying to put the man off guard.

"Well, good luck to him, mister! Ain't no concern o' mine, eh?"

The big man moved. With surprising agility in so large a man, he leapt on to the pelt.

"I bin enjoyin' sayin' my name,

friend. Dorrell, Dorrell, my name's Frankie Dorrell! Ain't bin able to say it for well on three years!" he burst out. "So now you know, an' it's time to say adios."

The trapper saw death in the black mouth of the .32 Harrington-Richardson levelled at his head.

"Shit, Mr Dorrell, I ain't stoppin' you sayin' your name. Go ahead an' say it as many times as you like," he yammered.

"Thank you sincerely, friend, I will. But I can't have you runnin' round sayin' you seen me, now can I?"

"Mister, I can't even remember *your* name; I've just forgot what you told me! Can't even remember seein' you!" the trapper gabbled.

Dorrell smiled coldly. "You sure won't!" The click as he cocked the gun had an icy finality.

"You was right about that cawfee, friend. It was real good!"

The grizzled head erupted in a shower of blood and bone shards as the Harrington-Richardson barked its message of death.

Dorrell stepped over the body and kicked the pelt aside to uncover the old Hawken. His eyes slitted as he beheld the dozens of notches on the stock, and the initials P.T.

"Mighty useful weapon, Mr P.T.," he muttered to himself, "Be a pity to let it rust away out here." He hefted the gun easily, shifting it from hand to hand. "You're a nice present. You an' me are gonna be real good for each other."

The heavy rifle slipped from his grasp and dropped on his foot, and he cursed long and loudly. If he'd guessed at the trouble the weapon would cause him, he'd have thrown it on the fire then and there . . .

Dorrell hummed cheerfully as he forked his palomino west.

"Massingham Town, here I come," he yelled, waving his Montana Peak at the sky. His thoughts ran to his ex-crony Wilbur Smallman who had a general store there. Well named at five feet six inches and a hundred and twenty pounds, Smallman had a pale, washed-out complexion and watery eyes. In fact, he was a bundle of energy, eating little yet trotting everywhere. In Lewis he'd been nicknamed Trotty, but anyone foolish enough to use the name in his hearing got thrashed soundly. He lived on the fringes of crime, mostly luring suckers to a rigged poker game.

Then one day he said, "Frankie, I'm pullin' up roots, gonna live in Massingham Town, find a wife 'n' settle down, start a family. I'm near fifty; had enough livin' on a knife edge." Nothing Dorrell could say changed his mind. Smallman grunted, "Massingham's peaceful; no guns allowed there. Plenty fellers would like to gun me down, so I'm off."

Later, when Dorrell had holed up in Santa Fe to escape the avenging Brack Bowman, he sent a letter by stage to Smallman but received no reply.

Now, hunching forward in his saddle, Dorrell smiled wolfishly.

No guns? Banks and no guns? All a man would have to do would be to slip a handgun into the town. Easy as pulling a nipple from a baby's mouth . . .

He thought of the sheriff whose name the town bore.

A tough customer with a reputation and a deputy who backed him up, but they didn't carry guns. He would hit the bank; then he'd have the money to pay high dollar gunnies, send 'em to Lewis to rub out Bowman. No more worries on that front. Brack Bowman, the self-styled avenger, was only one man. One against maybe six professional killers; it was like throwing a steak to a wolf-pack. Easy, yeah, easy!

2

DORRELL rode slowly, carefully examining the wire fence around the town. Sure, by itself it was no deterrent, but anyone who hadn't checked in his hardware at the gatehouse would soon run foul of Sheriff Massingham or his deputy. The deputy had a reputation, but that sheriff . . . at all costs he had to be avoided.

At a point where he couldn't be seen from the town, he nodded and smirked. He dismounted and bundled his gun into a piece of oilcloth, tied it firmly and left a long tail of stout twine. After burying the bundle just below the surface of the sandy soil, he pushed the tail of twine through the fence so that it rested beside a small log.

"Easy," he grunted, "I can pick it up just any time I want."

Inside the gatehouse, he smiled ingratiatingly whilst handing over the Hawken rifle. "Ever get any trouble from awkward customers, old-timer?" he asked as he pocketed a receipt in the name of 'Pete Towers'.

He complimented himself for inventing the name on the spur of the moment. Tom, the ancient gateman, chuckled wheezily, "Nope. When I rings this bell here on the wall it's the awkward cusses gets the trouble. Our young sheriff, nor his depity, don't take nonsense, no sir!"

Dorrell nodded approval. "Great. Firm sheriff is what makes a good town. Look after that rifle, won't you? Holds a lotta memories for me; I'm kinda attached to it," he lied.

Old Tom showed tobacco-yellowed teeth in a grin. "Sheriff Massingham's got one just like it. Mighty fine long range rifle, can kill a buffalo at a mile. Sure, it's old, but it's like me, does a fine job!"

With barely concealed annoyance

Dorrell allowed Tom to search him, quickly but efficiently. As he led his palomino to the stables, he could feel the old man's eyes follow him. "Silly old bastard," he muttered as he tugged the weary horse along.

After leaving the animal at the stable he strolled into the Lucky Star saloon to wash the dust from his throat. His ears wagged like an open barn door in a storm as he picked up information to store for future use. An hour later, wondering if his old crony Wilbur Smallman had found a wife and settled down, he was taking a bath at the Prairie Hotel.

"Gotta remember to tell him my name's Pete Towers nowadays," he muttered as he ran a hand over his unaccustomedly smooth skin. "Prob'ly won't recognize me," he grinned. "Used to have a face like a thorn bush."

He thought about it awhile, then looked at himself in the mirror. He wiped the steam off and peered more closely. "Yep," he opined, "You sure are a good lookin' feller, Peter Towers. That Dorrell worn't nothin' like as hansome!" He glanced at where his jacket hung, thinking of the bulge in his wallet since he'd emptied the murdered trapper's pockets. "And Dorrell," he mused contentedly, "worn't as rich as you either. When I've hit the bank, I'll be a mite richer still!"

He sniggered at his cunning. The initials P.T. on the Hawken might have meant anything, like 'Please Teacher' or 'Palomino's Testicles', any damned thing at all. It sure was smart to think up a name like Pete Towers.

He lay happy in his bed that night, listening to the wind gusting through the town. Dogs were howling in a way that in any other town would have earned them a few bullets; in Massingham Town folks could only shout at them.

The wind picked up until it was close to a gale, blowing down loose clapboard, hitching posts and dead trees. Branches tore away and crashed and buffeted along the ground. Dust hailed against windows and doors and sifted through every crack. A crocodile smile pulling at his face, Dorrell allowed the storm sounds to lull him off to sleep. Yes, he thought as he fell into his own darkness, This is one hell of a town, an' I'll have ev'ry last cent afore I go.

In her lonely bed old Mary Conlon smiled to herself. Sure, wouldn't there be plenty of kindling and small branches for her fire? Tis an ill wind that doesn't do no one any good. I'll have enough kindlin' to last me for months, she thought happily.

As daybreak came from a pearly salmon sky, she rose stiffly and put on a thick woollen dress and a man's slicker against the cold breeze. She walked slowly along inside the fence, her bright eyes missing nothing that could be used for her fire.

She struggled home with a heavy basket of kindling and a sack of small branches held down by a very nice little log. Praising the Lord for His bounty, she was quite unaware of the problem she would cause the man calling himself Pete Towers.

At midday Dorrell stamped into Jackson's saloon on West Side. He was hot and angry. Who in hell had taken that goddam log? The windblown sand had covered his length of twine and with the log gone there was no way he could find his weapon.

He felt as weak and unarmed as the two bit preacher man spouting religion outside the saloon. When he learned that Wilbur Smallman had returned to Lewis, his anger spilled over.

He flung his bulk into a secluded corner and pushed away the slim, pretty prostitute who appeared at his side.

"Clear off, you heap o' paint 'n' bones! Who in tarnation 'ud want a skinny rig like you? Ain't enough meat on you to make a jug o' stew!"

17

From the next booth came a retort, loud and clear. "And you, mister, have a fat gut an' enough fat between your ears to make stew for the entire nation!"

He stormed into the next booth. The setbacks of the day coupled with this insult set the blood coursing through his veins until his eyes started from his head.

It just wasn't his day.

The speaker rose languidly, seeming to go on uncoiling for ever. He was fully six feet five inches tall and his two hundred and ten pounds was plainly solid muscle and bone. Worst of all were the whip scars above and below ice-chip grey eyes which seemed to bore right through him. If Dorrell had any doubt as to the identity of the menacing figure confronting him, it vanished when he saw the sheriff's star glinting on his massive chest.

"Apologize to the lady, if you please."

Dorrell was no hero. There would

always be another day, or a dark night . . .

"Sorry, lady. I've had a rough day so far," he grated through clenched teeth.

The barman chuckled behind his counter. "Could've got a heap worse, mister! That's Sheriff Massingham you've upset."

Dorrell's trail-reddened eyes fell. "Sure sorry to upset you, Sheriff. Buy you a drink?"

Sheriff Massingham smiled tightly. "Thanks, but no. If I had a drink from every feller as upset me, I'd be no darned use to this town. But I'm sure the young lady would appreciate one. Name's Gloria, an' we all love her, don't we Gloria?"

Dorrell bit back the joke that rose to his lips. Although the sheriff was unarmed his fists were the size of four-pound rocks, and looked as hard.

Dorrell watched the sheriff duck his curly head as he shouldered his way through the batwings. "A bullet in the back of the head will stop that mother-f———— for sure," he promised himself savagely.

Returning greetings with a smile and a wave, the sheriff strolled to the gatehouse. His low-slung holster carried nothing more lethal than cigars and matches. On his battered office desk lay his Adams .44, a large calibre for such a lightweight weapon of just on a quarter of the Colt's weight. Not accurate at a distance, the Adams was ideal for a lightning draw in an eyeball to eyeball confrontation; a truth many a wrongdoer had discovered before meeting his Maker.

"Tom?" he called as he entered the gatehouse, "You here, y'old varmint?"

Tom popped up from behind the counter which ran the length of the room. He cursed fluently as his head connected with the gleaming brass bell on the wall. As the old man rubbed his bald pate, Massingham grinned at him affectionately.

"Will you stop ringin' that bell with

your head? I swear I never know if some jasper's givin' you a hard time, or it's you playin' the fool! Me'n Bert come runnin' — "

The gatekeeper scowled. "Have you come just to listen to your own tongue waggin'? Or have you got some business here, Sheriff?"

The sheriff grinned amiably; he knew how to handle Tom. "Mighty sorry to trouble you when you're workin', Tom." He scanned the room with the weapons neatly stacked on shelves. "Just wanted to talk hosses, Tom. But I'll come back when you ain't so busy."

"Now you just hold on, Sheriff. I'm somethin' of an hexpert on hosses, thought I told you that. Just ask away if you got any questions, young feller."

The sheriff smiled his thanks. "Mighty nice o' you, Tom."

Ten minutes later when they had finished discussing horses, the sheriff seized his chance. "By the way, Tom, that new feller in town. He booked in at the Prairie, name's Pete Towers, mind if I take a look at his hardware?"

"You're the sheriff, go ahead. That's his Winchester an' the Hawken. Seen some action, ain't it? I only hope those notches is for four-legged animals. Otherwise you got some kinda wild man in town."

The sheriff stared. "No handgun? Seems a mite funny to ride all that way an' not have a handgun. Seems — "

Tom butted in, a shrewd look in his eyes. "How'd you know he came a long ways? Bin lookin' at his hoss?"

Sheriff Massingham nodded as he hefted the Hawken, the spit image of his own.

"Yeah, I ran into him at Jackson's. Man's got a nasty mouth, an' a real mean streak. So I looked at his hoss. Wowee, Tom! Poor critter's mouth's damn near raw from being sawed with the reins, eyes rollin' like eggs in a fryin' pan, sweatin' an' near tuckered. If'n that ain't enough, near starved an' shoes worn right to hell. You know,

Tom, I don't like Mr Pete Towers worth a spit."

Tom nodded sagely. "This is a real good town. Way I see it is this: you don't like this jasper, an' he prob'ly don't love you much either. Now anywheres else it would prob'ly end up in a shootout, an' someone 'ud eat lead. Worst that can happen here is that someone'll get a mouthful o' fist, an' it ain't likely to be you on the receivin' end!"

The sheriff looked rueful. "Well, ain't never ate lead yet, but that miner sure gave a meal o' fist last year. Could only suck stuff for a week!" He shook his head. "Say Tom, you sure Towers hasn't sneaked a gun into town? It's been tried before."

The gatekeeper chuckled. "Waal son, I don't search fellers nowhere near as close as the ladies! But I checked him pretty good; don't think nothin' got past."

After a little more talk, Sheriff

Massingham took his leave and headed for his office. Catching sight of Martha Evans, he quickened his pace and pursed his lips as if lost in thought. A forlorn hope. Martha was the town gossip. Stories eddied around her in an on-rushing river of good news, bad news, and even more scandal and disaster. When the flow started to dry up, she wasn't above using her fertile imagination to set rumours flowing. Her sparse white hair fanned out behind her as she lurched straight towards the unfortunate sheriff.

He raised his hat resignedly. "Mornin', Martha. All well?" He cursed his inability to find an opener that would cut off further conversation as she planted her stumpy body right in front of him.

"There's mighty strange goin's on in this town, Sheriff. Jean Somers has been entertainin' that new teacher feller at night. He's been seen leavin' her place at all hours. 'Tain't decent! Her poor husband's only been dead two years, an' her in the Ladies Purity League."

Massingham smiled tightly. "It would surely be most improper behaviour if — "

She stomped her foot, her beaklike nose thrust up at him. "Would be? Darn well *is* improper, Sheriff. You got to do somethin'!"

Massingham tapped his chin pensively. "Yeah, reckon you're right, Martha. Someone 'ud better tell her brother. He'd be wilder than a stuck pig if he thought anyone was compromisin' the good Widow Somers. If people was blackenin' her name he could get real nasty. Kinda feller as lights up any lawyer's eyes."

His gravelly voice and the smile tugging at his lips should have warned her, but she plunged on regardless. Martha's tongue was always a yard ahead of her brain. "Brother? She ain't got no brother. What hogwash you talk, young Massingham."

"Waal, Martha, that may be so, but

25

John Rivers is her brother. Somers is her married name. Know the feller? The New Englander who came here last month; the new school teacher!"

He paused to let the words sink in. "Waal, Martha. Sure glad we cleared that up. Can't have those nasty old gossips at the LPL gettin' themselves sued for slander, now can we?"

Mortified that her latest titbit of gossip had soured in her mouth, she had the grace to blush. However, Massingham wasn't going to escape so easily.

"Well, what about that feller that rode in yesterday? Funny lookin' cuss, that one."

Anything about the so-called Pete Towers concerned the sheriff; his nose told him the man was nothing but trouble.

"Biggish feller in a city suit, ridin' a sorry lookin' palomino?"

Her eyes gleamed with triumph. "That's the one . . . I couldn't sleep last night for the wind." She paused, taking time to polish her story.

Massingham couldn't help cutting in, "Sure sorry to hear you suffer that way, Martha. Wind can be a big trial, they tell me."

She suspected he was making fun of her and flared up irascibly, "No, you young fool! The storm, didn't you hear the storm last night?"

"No Martha," he lied, "I got an easy conscience so I sleep well. But if there was a storm, I don't see as I can do much about it. The Good Lord sends us — "

She screeched, "I don't want you to arrest the Good Lord! Listen to what I'm tellin' you. I got up early because I thought the weather would bring down a little extra kindlin'. That miserable wretch Mary Conlon beat me to it! Got all the best stuff — "

Massingham was enjoying himself. "Ah, I see. You want me to take Mary Conlon in. What'd be the charge, Martha?"

She glared at him. "Could you shut

27

up a minute, Sheriff? That feller who came in on the palomino was up early too. Walkin' round inside the fence like he was tryin' to find some kindlin' for hisself. But Mary had it all. He sure looked cross. Now, Sheriff, why would he want kindlin'? Don't our hotel have any water heatin'?"

Massingham's brain was racing . . . What in God's name? . . . Unless he'd planted a gun to be picked up later; it had been tried before.

Extracting himself from Martha's clutches, he hurried to his office, and found Bert, his part-time deputy, just emerging.

"Hi Bert, lookin' for me?"

As well as being the call-out deputy, Bert worked at the Prairie. Since he didn't wear his badge at the hotel, he tended to pick up valuable information. His thin, round-shouldered stance, his droopy moustache and worried frown, took strangers in. He could straighten those shoulders to produce a fast draw, and he'd once come first in the carnival rifle shooting competition.

"Yep. Funny thing happened yesterday, Mass. Feller signed in at the Prairie, called hisself Pete Towers."

"And?"

Bert scratched his head. "When I looked in the book, I saw he'd torn out a sheet an' thrown it in the basket. He'd started to write *Frankie Dorr—* , then crossed it out before he threw it away. Then he wrote Pete Towers in the book."

"That feller's up to no good, Bert," Massingham grunted, then told his deputy all he knew of the stranger.

Bert nodded thoughtfully. "Scouting round the fence, huh? Looks like you're right; he must've hidden a gun outside the fence, then tried to haul it in, the way that Garwood jasper did. Not that he lived long enough to benefit, eh?"

The rangy sheriff mopped his brow with a blue bandanna and grinned sardonically. "Nope. But he cost me two shells before that brother-in-law o' yours could rub his hands."

It was a standing joke between them that the undertaker complained of impoverishment since the no-gun law. Massingham interrupted his deputy's laughter.

"Say Bert, he's got an ol' Hawken with near fifty notches on the stock, plus the initials P.T. Now we both know the .60 is the sorta gun trappers use. So how come Mr Towers in his city suits owns both a Hawken and a Winchester? An' if'n his name ain't Pete Towers, as you suspect, how'd he get his hands on it, an' why?"

Bert sucked on his droopy bootlace moustache a while, then opined, "P'raps he bought it like you did your'n. But it don't make sense him not totin' a handgun."

They stood in the sun, tipping their hats when ladies passed, and talking easily. But both lawmen had a nagging suspicion that this stranger was trouble . . .

"Gotta get back to the Prairie, Mass. Y'know I almost wish that jasper could get his hands on a gun; least we'd know where we was then, eh?"

★ ★ ★

That evening Massingham called on Martha Evans. If anyone would know what the stranger had been doing, it would be Martha, he told himself with a grin.

He was right. It seemed the stranger had walked all the way round town, over the little bridge that divided it; then he'd circled the bank three times. He'd stood looking over the batwings into the Lucky Star saloon for several minutes, and she hadn't seen him since.

"I've got other things to do," she finished tartly.

Massingham thanked her and left. She'd confirmed his gut feeling about the stranger, but where was the man going to get a gun? Did he intend to steal one from the gatehouse? Or did he have a friend in town who just might have a gun hidden somewhere? It seemed certain that he'd stashed a gun just outside the fence, planning to haul it in later, but now that had gone wrong would he just up and go quietly?

He made his evening rounds, spending time to chat with townsfolk, glancing in saloon bars to check that all was well, before engaging in earnest conversation with his old friend ex-Sheriff Roy Greensleaves.

Roy retired when he'd been crippled by a gunnie named Slim Gaunt. Massingham had soon caught up with the man to give him his just deserts. The ex-sheriff now ran the recently installed telegraph office. Massingham moved with his lithe, easy pace that ate up the ground. He stopped on the little bridge to gaze at the water and watch a few hammerheads plopping as they pursued moths and gnats. Once he'd saved this water from the evil half Mex half Chinese Ganzo, and in doing so he'd nearly lost his life.

The townsfolk had then voted that the town's name be changed to Massingham Town. Since that memorable day a lot of water had flowed under the bridge. He rubbed his chin; then his fingers dropped to stroke a gold medallion hanging on a chain round his neck.

The medallion had been dented by Ganzo's bullet in a shoot-out before the assembled town. He shook his head, dismissing the memories, then strolled to Jackson's to order a small beer which he drank reclining in a booth.

He'd almost finished the drink when the batwings swung inwards and the man who called himself Towers entered and bellied up to the bar. Having invested the murdered trapper's money in a smart grey suit and a haircut, he looked considerably smarter.

Massingham stepped up quietly behind him.

"Evenin', Towers. Join me?"

Dorrell nodded. "Sure thing, Sheriff. I'll have same's you; what's good 'nuff for you is good 'nuff for me. After all, it's your town."

"Sure is. Two beers, Sam."

They talked, smoked and drank their beer. Massingham found his companion tight-lipped about himself but deeply interested in the town and how it was run. As he carefully laid a trap, the sheriff smiled inwardly; he'd catch this jasper out and no one would get hurt.

He was now convinced that the man was out to get a gun and rob the bank. No other interpretation of what Martha had said was possible; he certainly wasn't in town to kill anyone.

At quarter to ten the sheriff bade Dorrell goodnight before returning to his office to meet Bert. By ten o'clock they were sitting with their feet up on the office table, busy comparing notes. At the same moment Dorrell was leaning over the parapet of the bridge and gazing at the water as Massingham had done earlier that evening.

He let out a raucous guffaw. "A real crazy, one-eyed town! Wide open to a man with a brain an' a gun."

Once more he laughed gratingly. "An' thanks to that dumb sheriff who don't know when to keep his trap shut, I know where I'll get my hardware."

The more he thought about it, the better it looked. The sheriff might be a fast gun, when he'd got one! But his brain seemed to have gone on a round-up; it sure wasn't in his head.

3

BERT shook his head doubtfully. "Don't really think this jasper'll break in here to take our guns, do you?"

"I watched his eyes, Bert. He sure as hell will. Bet you a quart o' whisky to a pinch o' hoss shit! His eyes just lit up when I told him the hardware was kept on this table by day. I led him on real good, told him the council didn't like the idea at first, all the truth with a little pinch o' extra here an' there. Musta jawed his ears off. He hardly said a word 'cept for an odd crafty question."

In truth the sheriff's idea for a gun-free town had been coolly received at first. Then some people argued it should apply to the lawmen; so they agreed to leave their guns where they could be easily collected, handguns in the office, rifles at the gatehouse. However, the lawmen insisted on taking the handguns home at night.

A number of bells had been placed around town so that the lawmen could be summoned by ringing one. Six months jail was the penalty for ringing a bell without cause. It worked excellently. Many tough gunmen were delighted to find somewhere to drink and play cards, without the past creeping up to put a bullet in them, or having to deal with some young fool trying to make a reputation.

As he recalled the man's attempt, staring fixedly into his beer glass, to contain his growing excitement, the sheriff chuckled. He'd told the stranger truthfully that the gatehouse was manned each day by old Tom, and by night an Englishman (who slept days because of a reaction to the sun) took over.

"Sheriff," he'd said, the glee lurking in his voice, "Seems a lotta trouble for you havin' to dash back for your hardware when some feller's got a gun. Bit risky too, eh?"

"Would be, Mr Towers, if'n it happened regular. But once I put three guys in the ground, an' my ole deputy blasted two halfway to Mexico, things seemed to go real quiet. I gotta watch we don't put ourselves outa a job!"

So Dorrell had swallowed the bait. Now Bert was listening to the sheriff with a half smile tugging at his lips. Then a seed of doubt broke open in his eyes.

He shook his head. "OK, Mass, so he steals our guns — "

"No, Sunshine, not *our* guns; a pair we've left out for him. *Ours* will be safe in our keeping, for once."

His deputy stared at him in disbelief and chewed on his moustache. "Can't believe what I'm hearin', Mass. You lookin' for a shoot-out? S'pose he kills someone first, like the bank manager? Sounds risky to me."

Massingham gave him the dark smile

that always sent shivers skittering up his spine.

"No chance. The guns'll be fixed so the hammers don't reach the caps."

"Massingham, you're turnin' into a prize bastard. You're talkin' about murderin' this guy, 'cause that's what it amounts to."

The sheriff yawned and stretched. "Nobody's gonna die, less'n you an' me die laughin' when he tries to gun us down! Like it?"

Bert looked vastly relieved. "But how are we gonna know when he's robbed the bank? Where are we at the time?"

"Roy Greensleeves will watch the bank from 'cross the road at the telegraph office. He'll ring his bell when Towers comes out. Should be just a mite entertainin'," the sheriff drawled.

Bert grinned. "More'n a mite. But it'll be adios for you if'n that jasper gets away with the money. This town'll feed your liver to the dogs. But it's worth the risk!"

Bert threw across a fat cigar, and the two men leaned back for a contented smoke. The sheriff watched his deputy through eyes slitted against the blue smoke. Bert seemed like a cat before a saucer of cream.

"What're you so all-fired cheery about, Mr Deputy? Hopin' it'll go wrong so you can get my job?" he teased.

Bert expelled two perfect smoke rings. "Had a kinda sneaky look through Mr Towers' belongin's, Mass."

The sheriff recoiled in feigned horror. "Hey, Bert, how could you do such a thing? Ain't lawful rummagin' through a man's things." He grinned broadly. "Come on, then. What did you find?"

"Little ole receipt coupla years old, faded. Stuck right in the corner o' his bag."

"A receipt! That a hangin' offence, Bert?"

"Shut up, Mass! He bought a hoss over to Lewis; his name's Frankie Dorrell."

Massingham chuckled and shook his head. "He's got a hoss named Frankie Dorrell? Kinda fancy name — "

Bert sighed deeply. "I can see you're in one o' them moods, Mass. You don't get no better."

"Can't help it, Bert. Waitin' to see this jasper's face when he draws on us is just killin' me. So you reckon his name's Frankie Dorrell. Proves what you suspected when he signed the Prairie register. We better get Roy to telegraph Lewis an' see if'n they got anythin' on a Towers or a Dorrell."

Bert slapped his thigh in annoyance. "Forgot to tell you somethin' else. There was one o' those crazy dime cowboy books in his bag. Sort that makes 'em look mean an' fast on the draw, an' they can all shoot the ticks off'n a grizzly's balls at half a mile."

The sheriff laughed. "Yeah, rubbish. They can't all shoot like you, Bert! But am I supposed to charge him with readin' trash?"

Bert winced. "Ain't the sorta book

that matters. It's the shop stamp on the back that looks interestin'. 'Robinson's Cabin Store, *Santa Fe*.' An it looks pretty new to me."

Massingham tossed his cigar butt into a can by the door; he could do it with his eyes shut. "So you figure he left Lewis some time ago, an' went to Santa Fe. Then he rode right back to little ole Massingham Town. So what've we got in this town that's so darned special, Bert?"

Bert lit a fresh cigar and pointed with it at Massingham.

"A town without guns. Martha said he's bin lookin' at the bank a lot. You reckon he was searchin' round the fence like he was huntin' for a gun. He's asked you a lotta questions. When he gets a gun we'll know what it's about."

Massingham stood. "That's about it, Bert. So if'n you hang on here, I'll have Archie fix a coupla guns for us."

Archie was the gunsmith. The

townsfolk had guns which they kept at the gatehouse and picked up when they went out of town. Some keen riflemen often got into a little gully to practise for the Carnival competition and the lawmen practised their fast draws and tricks each week.

Although it was late in the evening, Archie was still tinkering in the back of his shop when the sheriff arrived.

"Ain't much business these days, Sheriff. Me an' the undertaker might's well leave town," he grunted.

Massingham lowered his frame onto an upturned shell box, and grinned amiably, "Think yourself lucky you got a share in the stables; undertaker's only got corpses to keep him alive!"

When the sheriff had finished explaining his idea, Archie slapped his ample thigh in delight. "Simple. Two spiked guns. What a laugh! Should be worth seein'," he chortled.

"Archie, I know I can rely on you to say nothing. Bert an' me reckon he's goin' to try to rob the bank. So, less'n you got a grudge against me an' Bert, you make sure them guns don't work!"

The gunsmith laughed until his face was red and sweating. "I'm gonna enjoy fixin' them guns real good," he gasped. "Wish I could see that guy's face when he pulls the triggers. Sure you wouldn't like me to fix 'em so's they explode in his hands? 'Tain't no trouble."

Massingham looked sombre. "No thanks, Archie. Don't want no one gettin' hurt. 'Sides, I don't want no judge gettin' sympathetic an' lettin' him off light. This character travels under different handles, an' if'n I know anythin' 'bout men, he's real bad."

The sheriff's face was set in granite lines, and Archie shivered. Massingham was a hard man to cross; even when he'd only been a boy he'd killed two men intent on molesting his mother.

"I'll bring 'em round, prob'ly before nine o'clock, OK?"

The sheriff's face softened, "You're a good man, Archie, an' a real pal. Wrap 'em up; can't have no one ringin' a bell 'cos of seein' you carryin' guns!"

"Want 'em loaded, Sheriff?"

Massingham nodded grimly. "Loaded an' all ready to fire; but if'n they do fire, I'll come back an' haunt you!"

On returning to the office, he found Bert checking and oiling their guns. These days Bert favoured a Colt, but the sheriff stuck to his old lightweight Adams .44. They left the office and, as they always did at night, holstered their guns to take home.

Bert was pulling distractedly at his moustache, "Does that jasper know there ain't no guns here at night? An' how's he goin' to get into the place in the day?"

The sheriff smiled easily, "Bert, my brain ain't dried up yet! I told him the guns go home with us at night. Then I told him I eat lunch with you at Jackson's at midday. I said it was essential to have a good midday meal and rest a coupla hours. So he thinks we're out the way at least two hours. Prob'ly hopes service is as bad as at the Prairie, which would keep us away half the day!"

This last was to tease Bert who was inordinately proud of the hotel where he spent most of his time.

Bert grinned sourly, "That reminds me, he's seen me at the Prairie. So I'd better not be seen by him in your company. He could smell a rat."

The sheriff nodded, "Yep, we better keep apart awhiles; meet up accidental in the stables, say eleven in the mornin'?"

Bert grinned broadly, "Sounds real romantic, Mass, an' there's me thinkin' you were keen on Martha Evans!"

"Real funny Mr Deputy. Any more questions?"

"Yeah, Mass. You ain't told me how he's gonna get in."

Massingham smiled, "Ever looked at the lock an' chain on this door? A baby could pry 'em apart with a spoon. So long, Sunshine. See you at the stables in the mornin.'"

★ ★ ★

Frankie Dorrell was propped up in bed reading a dime novel about cowboys. A smart businessman had realized the legend of the West could be big business and started publishing highly romanticized stories of the alleged cowboy way of life.

The publisher was amazed to discover that, far from being irked by this, real cowboys revelled in this spurious image. They tried hard to copy the walk and style of their heroes, although unfortunately they hadn't the money to buy the accoutrements needed. Often they borrowed clothes to pose for photographs which they sent to their families. There were even some who shot off their toes trying the fast draw. Fast on the trigger, slow on the draw. One writer, a Colonel Ingraham, later turned out over a hundred cheap novels about Buffalo Bill Cody. These stories gave impetus to the Wild West shows which were fast becoming popular.

Dorrell's thoughts kept slipping back to the sheriff's office where the guns were kept, and that cute little one-man bank not far off. He threw down his novel, and let a grin spread over his face.

No rush, he told himself, take your time Frankie boy. You know the sheriff an' his depity eat at midday. But you must see the scar-faced bastard again, check it out, just drop it into conversation. Yes! Call round tomorrow an' report that crazy ole woman who keeps follerin' you round like a dog. What in hell's she up to? His mind went on circling until he muttered aloud, "What in hell's it matter 'bout the ole witch? She's givin' me a chance to see the sheriff."

He slept deeply but woke unrefreshed. What in hell was the nightmare about? Something involving the trapper and his gun? The old gatehouse keeper too ... He seemed to be gabbling something Dorrell couldn't quite understand.

He felt his skin lift and crawl, as if someone had walked over his grave.

4

SHORTLY after 8.30 in the morning Archie came into the sheriff's office with a bundle under his arm. "Here y'are, Massingham, two Smith & Wessons that look like the real thing, only they ain't no use to anyone!"

Massingham unwrapped the weapons and pointed them at the gunsmith's chest. "Thanks Archie. Bet your hide they can't be fired?"

Archie nodded his shining pate vigorously, "Sure, go ahead an' try 'em."

The sheriff winked and pointed the guns at the ceiling. "Ain't no man knows more 'bout guns than you, old friend. But you're too valuable to this town. Can't chance it, you might've made your first mistake, eh?"

There were two clicks as the sheriff

triggered the pistols.

"Hammers not reachin' the caps, Archie? That what you said you'd do?" he enquired.

"You betcha they ain't, Mass. There's no way them guns can be fired."

Massingham placed a huge hand on the gunsmith's shoulder.

"I owe you one, Archie. I won't forget," he avowed.

Archie blushed with pleasure. "Dang it, Sheriff. Me'n the rest of the town owe you more'n we can ever repay. I ain't forgettin' how you stood up to that bastard Ganzo who was stealin' our water. Ever' time I see you with that dented medallion round your neck I bless God for you."

After the gunsmith had left Massingham slipped his .44 Adams into the pocket of an old slicker hanging behind the door. He placed the two useless weapons on the desk and lit his first cigar of the day.

He'd just shaken out the match when Martha Evans bustled into the office.

She came straight to the point. "Sheriff, that feller's just walked round the bank another three times. Last night he walked along inside the fence again, and then outside. He was kicking at the ground an' swearing so's I had to cover my ears!"

Massingham suppressed a grin. "You sure he was swearin', Martha? I mean, how could a lady member of the League for Purity — ?"

She glared at him, "Don't you start makin' fun of me, Sheriff!"

He shook his head solemnly, "Wouldn't think of it, Martha."

She watched him suspiciously, then continued, "All of a sudden, he laughed out loud and shouted like he was drunk, 'You're going to help me, Massingham, you're going to help me!' . . . "

Massingham's smile was dark and cold. "Don't tell anyone Martha, but he could just be right."

She almost gobbled, "You'd help that creature, Massingham? How on earth — ?"

Massingham chuckled softly. "Yeah. If'n he wanted to blow his head off I'd load the gun for him, or I'd sharpen his razor for him if'n he wanted to cut his throat! He's bad news, Martha, an' I'll give him enough rope to hang himself, OK?"

She rose and held out a wrinkled hand. "Thank you Massingham. Will you need me to — ?"

"No thank you, ma'am. Wouldn't want him to suspect anythin', would we? But I won't forget as it was you put me onto the varmint. Your warnin' has been invaluable to this town."

★ ★ ★

Massingham was checking the Smith and Wessons. Well oiled and gleaming darkly, their blue-black sheen appeared to promise death. He grinned and shook his head; the guns would kill nobody. When he looked up, Frankie Dorrell, alias Pete Towers, was leaning in the doorway watching him like a cat studying a bird.

"Mornin', Sheriff Them the only guns in town, eh? Looks like you treat 'em real well."

"You're right there. These guns've been well treated," Massingham replied with an ingenuous smile. "They live here all day an' go home with me an' my depity nights. They don't hardly do no work at all! Only used 'bout once a week for practice down the gully. But then I told you that, didn't I? What can I do for you, mister?"

Dorrell ambled in and plonked down on a stool. Hunched over, he had the appearance of a bird of prey balanced on a rock. He sat with his hands under him, and his sharp little eyes darted round the room taking in details.

"Sounds kinda silly, Sheriff," he said at length, "But someone's been follerin' me, every darned place I go. I want you — "

Massingham shook his head in mock disbelief, "Everywhere?"

"Just about, an' it's gotta be stopped."

Massingham tipped back his hat and frowned.

"Got a description? This feller might be — "

Dorrell cut across him, "Not a feller, a darned woman."

Massingham looked at him admiringly, "Well now, lotta guys'd find that real dandy. You must have some secret attraction, Mr Towers. If'n you could bottle it, you could make a fortune outa that!"

The other man's face flushed dangerously as he pushed back his stool. Massingham's eyes watched him like chips of grey ice, and he sank back onto it.

"Shit, she ain't no beauty, just a stumpy ole witch!"

The sheriff leaned towards him, man to man.

"Ain't no tellin' with women, an' when they get old they sometimes get worse. I think you must be talkin' 'bout Martha Evans; she's harmless enough."

"You know her? What in hell's the

matter with her? She loco?"

Massingham sighed, and lit a cigar to head off the laughter bubbling up in him. "Man mad," he whispered, "She was left at the altar three times, took to gin. Tags along after any good-lookin' feller who comes to town, but stops after a few days. Usually."

Dorrell had finished sizing up the room. The old door lock and chain would bust off easily.

The sheriff had noticed his eyes slipping round every corner; he guessed the real purpose of the man's visit.

"So you want me to arrest her? Or maybe just caution her? She musta really fell for you."

Somehow Dorrell contained his anger. This bastard sheriff, he thought, is makin' fun o' me. Never mind, he'll stop grinnin' when he looks down the wrong end o' his own hardware! I'll sure as hell treat myself to that little pleasure afore I leave . . ."

"Nah, Sheriff, just thought I'd mention it."

He rose heavily and held out his hand.

Massingham ignored it.

Dorrell's face darkened. You got a nice peaceful little town here. Sure hope it stays that way, but then nothin' ever does, does it?"

Massingham answered flintily, "It'll stay the same while I'm alive, Mr Towers. So you're safe here less'n you get to fist fightin'."

Frankie Dorrell emerged from the office, blinking in the sunlight and with mixed feelings. He was pleased with his reconnaissance but fuming at the sheriff. It was like the damned man was not only mocking him but saw inside his head. He shivered involuntarily . . . "Still," he consoled himself, "Bastard can be tougher'n a grizzly but he'll still be cold meat when the bullets tear his guts. Things are gonna change quicker'n you think, Sheriff. Right after I've hit the bank I'll put a bullet or two through you, ride back to Vengo an' pick up a few gunslingers. They'll take care o' Brack Bowman in Lewis, while I head into Mexico with the gold. Hang on awhiles, señoritas, I'm comin'!"

He hummed through his teeth as he sauntered into the Lucky Star.

"Set 'em up, barman. Drinks're on me," he offered with a wave of a newly purchased silk handkerchief.

The man shot him a lopsided smile, "You sure know how to choose your time, mister. There's only the two o' us here!"

Dorrell nodded and patted his sweating brow with the handkerchief, "That's the secret o' life, barman; it's all down to timin'. Know what you wanta do, an' do it at the right time; that's all there is to it."

"Easy as that, eh?" the barman muttered as he wiped down the counter.

"Yeah," Dorrell affirmed as he gulped back his drink.

As the fiery liquid caught at his throat, he spluttered and coughed.

The silk handkerchief made a fresh appearance as he mopped the front of his new suit.

The barman grinned sardonically, "Yep, I reckon it's all 'bout timin', mister. A man has to get his timin' right!"

5

WHEN Massingham strolled into the stables Bert was waiting for him.

"Well, Mass, what's new?" the deputy enquired eagerly.

The sheriff lowered his rangy frame onto a bale of straw, and patted the slicker he carried over his arm.

"Got my Adams in here; you'd better hold on to your Peacemaker. That jasper called round to spy out the land. He sure was taken with them Smith and Wessons o' Archie's! Damn near ready to eat 'em."

As usual, Bert looked worried and a little puzzled.

"But Mass, are we gonna just sit back an' let him rob the bank? Or let the manager blow his damn head off?"

"Bert," Massingham said straight-faced, "If'n that bank manager has a gun, my deputy ain't doin' his job, is he?"

The deputy shook his head slowly, "So, OK, he goes to the bank with the spiked guns. What then?"

The sheriff grinned. "Roy sees from the telegraph office. He rings the bell as the guy comes out, and we pick him up with the loot."

Bert allowed a rare smile to cross his features, "Martha still trailin' him round town?"

Massingham nodded, "He came an' reported it! I told him she was man mad, jilted three times at the altar!"

Bert screwed up his face, "Kinda overdoin' it, ain't you?"

The sheriff merely chuckled.

Bert looked serious once more, "All the same, maybe we should warn the bank manager. Don't want him havin' a heart attack, do we?"

Massingham looked thoughtful. "Guess you're right, Bert. Will you drop by an' warn him? Explain the guns don't work, but tell him to look scared as hell just the same."

Bert looked relieved. "Sure, I'll do that. But when do you reckon he's goin' to try to pull this thing? We'll have to keep outa sight so's he doesn't smell a rat, but we can't hang round waitin' forever."

The sheriff produced two cigars from his holster, lit one and handed the other to his deputy. He blew a perfect smoke ring over Bert's head. "Beat that! I reckon midday tomorrow, when I'm feedin' my face at Jackson's."

"Won't go pluggin' him when he draws, will you?" Bert asked sombrely. "He might as well be unarmed."

The sheriff laughed affectionately, "Relax, you ole worry-guts. When he looks down the wrong end of our guns just after his have gone CLICK, CLICK, he'll be the one havin' heart failure! Save the cost of tryin' him, won't it?"

Bert permitted himself a second smile, "Should be good to see. Less'n it goes wrong; then we'd be in it up to our necks!"

The sheriff punched his shoulder, "Relax, what can go wrong?"

★ ★ ★

Bert was whistling at his work in the Prairie as he thought of his talk with Monty Upton at the bank.

Monty had seemed inordinately intrigued and excited by the whole thing; then Bert recalled that he'd come over from England with the gold rush. As an actor on hard times, he'd found the lure of the rush impossible to resist. He'd failed miserably and, because he'd a flair for figures, he turned to banking. When he reached Massingham Town, his appearance and manner inspired confidence. Acting scared for the benefit of the bogus Pete Towers had caught his imagination; as Bert unrolled the plan, Monty's blue eyes had sparkled with excitement.

As he bustled about Bert noticed another dime novel left by a visitor. The plot unfolding around him was better than any book. To trick a man who was likely an outlaw into stealing guns, robbing a bank and walking into the arms of the law. Then, as the guy tried to blast his way out, he'd find that the guns wouldn't work . . .

Bert's natural moroseness surfaced . . . Suppose the man did get away with the money? What if it all went wrong? Hell no! Massingham wouldn't let this character slip through his fingers; no one had ever got the better of him yet! Why should this man be the first?

★ ★ ★

Monty gazed at the mirror on the wall of his office at the bank.

Reflected back at him was the image of a suntanned, bald-headed man of around fifty, tall and spare. The glasses on his long, sensitive face were hornrimmed with plain lenses. The unneeded spectacles gave him an air of studious respectability and were a great asset in his work. However, his heart was still in the theatres of London; acting stays in the blood, and banking provided scant opportunity to get his adrenalin flowing.

Now he had a great chance to act the part of a terrified bank manager facing the death-dealing guns of a brutal robber.

Oh what fun he'd have! With absolutely no danger . . . He checked his watch. It had to be soon, he'd burst if he had to wait much longer. His happiness was marred only by the knowledge that his audience would be limited to one. Nevertheless, he'd give of his best, and what a performance he'd put on!

★ ★ ★

Massingham was quite sure that Dorrell would make his move at midday. The only question in the sheriff's mind was which day? Tomorrow or the day after? Today would be too soon for him to get ready.

He decided to visit Roy Greensleaves at the telegraph office.

He and Roy shared a house on the west side of town, the house in which Roy was to have lived with Massingham's widowed mother. When Rita was murdered Roy had invited Massingham to sell the farmhouse in which he lived and move in with him. The arrangement worked well and the ex-sheriff was a valued confidante and adviser.

As he sank into one of Roy's office chairs, the young sheriff made the frame creak ominously. At the prospect of a talk, Roy's face brightened.

"Hi, son," he said, "Make yourself comfortable. Break up my chairs if'n you feel that way. Coffee's brewed, help yourself."

Massingham poured into a large, chipped mug. He took a sip and smacked his lips in appreciation.

"Best brew in town, Roy," he observed.

Roy smiled at him amiably, "Free

too! To what momentous events do I owe this honour?"

Massingham produced a cigar and lit it carefully.

Roy shook his head in mock dismay, "Shit Mass! You'll stunt your growth if'n you keep smokin' them things!"

"So you keep tellin' me. Bert an' me were talkin' 'bout that new jasper at the Prairie. Got some more to tell you; then maybe you can think up somethin' more I can do."

Massingham quickly brought Roy up to date. The older man listened without interruption. When Massingham finished, Roy picked up his walking stick and balanced it across his knees like a shotgun.

"OK, son, you reckon to nail him for breakin' into your office, stealin' guns, bein' in possession of guns in this town, hopefully with robbin' the bank, then with attempted murder of yourself an' maybe Bert. Am I right so far?"

Massingham steepled his fingers, "Absolutely."

Roy grinned and pointed at him with the walking stick, "Hope them guns've been fixed real good, son."

Massingham drained his coffee, "Yeah, Archie fixed 'em an' I tried 'em. Had 'em fixed so's he couldn't plug Monty Upton or no one else. I wasn't fixin' to back down, you understand?"

Roy chuckled, "An there was me thinkin' you'd suddenly gone yeller!"

Massingham pursed his lips in irritation, "I just aim to see him danglin' on the end o' a rope! I'm sure we're gonna find this feller's a murderin' coyote. He'll be wanted somewhere, or my name ain't Massingham!"

Roy swung his stick in a whistling arc, "Guess you're right, son. Want me to wire round a bit? Slade Town, Lewis, Tarnville, Yellowsnake? Maybe Santa Fe? If'n you're right, man's sure to have a record. Might take a while but I'll find it. What the telegraph's for, ain't it?"

Massingham lifted his hat and

scratched his head, "It sure took long enough to reach these parts; began to think they'd forgotten us." He tried to blow a smoke ring, failed, tried again and stubbed his cigar out on the sole of one of his soft, calf length boots.

"Better get in some practice," he muttered, and grinned to himself.

Roy rose to the bait. "Yeah, stick with the practice, son. Blast away in that gully! Your life could depend on it!"

Massingham let a wide smile spread across his face. "What you talkin' 'bout, Roy? One minute you're sayin' stop smokin' cigars or it'll stunt your growth; next you say don't forget to practise as much as you can!"

Roy looked mystified, "Sheriff's flipped his lid!"

"Roy, I meant smoke rings. Gotta practise or that darned depity o' mine'll keep on beatin' me at it, an' that ain't fittin'!"

Roy shook his head, "Poke fun at a poor old man! But make sure you come runnin' when I ring that bell, or you'll be up to your medallion in hoss shit! Now get outa here an' let me get on with my work, you schemin' sonofabitch. You know, you get more like Ole Nick every day."

Massingham sauntered back to his office, thinking it would be splendid if Roy came up with the goods on the stranger. Still, one way or another the law would catch up with the man.

It was just on midday when he let himself into the office; he was going to make sure the man tried nothing that day. It would be better to wait until the telegraph came up with something before springing the trap. Tomorrow would be soon enough. He wasn't at all surprised when the man appeared in the doorway, his bulky figure blocking out the light.

"Saw the door open, Sheriff," the stranger drawled. "Eatin' over to Jackson's? I'll walk over with you an' grab a bite myself."

Yeah sure, Massingham thought;

then you'll make some bullshit excuse to leave, an' that would be that . . .

"Nice o' you to ask, Mister — " He bit back 'Dorrell' and added, "Towers. But I clean forgot to tell you I don't eat Wednesdays. Catch up on my paperwork. Sorry, so if'n you don't mind — ?"

Dorrell nodded, his eyes sliding to the gleaming guns. "Sure, very conscientious o' you, Sheriff. Maybe see you at Jackson's tomorrow, eh?"

"You'll see me for sure tomorrow," Massingham replied levelly.

Yeah, for sure, Dorrell thought delightedly, less'n you get very lucky, you scar-faced bastard.

At Jackson's Dorrell ordered a steak and a bottle of wine. He smirked as he thought of the trapper's purse from which he'd soon pay. All them critters he shot, an' all for me! Wonder if'n all them notches on that Hawken was buffalo. Grizzlies? Cougars? Must be fifty notches an' in the end it come to me, all five hundred dollars! Enough to buy some new clothes, a few steaks, plenty booze, an' maybe a nice plump whore. He liked them that way. With plenty of meat, they were better able to stand the kind of punishment he liked to dish out.

His thoughts returned to the sheriff; the bastard had nearly hit him over that gal in the bar. "I'll sure pay you for that tomorrow, Sheriff," he whispered.

He ran over his plans for the next day. In the morning he'd pick up a good horse at the stables, bit more life in it than that bastard palomino. Then hitch it outside the telegraph office so's not to arouse suspicion. In the telegraph office he'd enquire if there was anything for him; not that there would be. He stroked his nose with a thick forefinger. Have to take a peek from the telegraph office window to see if the sheriff was on his way to feed his face. As soon as the lawman was out of the way Dorrell would break the lock off his office door with a small piece of iron rod. The Smith & Wessons would go into a grip and be toted to the bank. The plans were foolproof!

Forking steak into his mouth and knocking back wine, he chortled softly. He was far too smart for this one-eyed town and its two bit sheriff!

The rest of his plans looked as good. Paying gunslingers with the money from the bank to take care of Bowman . . . Just for an instant the name of the self-styled avenger sent shivers rippling down his spine. Bowman had plenty of reasons for vengeance. Hadn't he back-shot John Bowman? Thank God, he thought, I'll be able to take care of him without going anywhere near him.

A disagreeable thought struck him and he paused in the act of chewing. What if he killed the damned sheriff? Lawmen had a way of looking after their own; they'd track him down like a one-legged buffalo.

Shit! he thought. I'd've enjoyed rubbin' out that Sheriff bloody Massingham. But it wouldn't be smart; I'd just swop one avenger from Lewis for an army from Massingham Town, an' other lawmen'd join in. Nah, it'd be just plain dumb, killin' a sheriff!

He went on chewing and gulped down the steak which now felt and tasted like old boot leather with a glass of wine. Well, he consoled himself, if the sheriff turned up unexpectedly a bullet through each leg would hold him up a mite. They weren't going to send out a goddam army for that, surely?

Again he felt coldness flow over him. Hadn't the trapper said Bowman was a lawman? He swilled more wine. What the hell? What was there to connect him with Bowman when *hired gunnies* shot him down? Nothing!

It was all going to work out just fine, wasn't it?

6

IN the absence of Sheriff Howe, Brack Bowman sat at a desk of gargantuan proportions, a gift from an old lady. Sheriff Howe hadn't the heart to refuse it, but it took up most of the office and left little room for the two lawmen, their chairs, two small stools and a wall cabinet.

In build and temperament Sheriff Massingham and the Lewis deputy were very alike. Massingham was distinguished by the two whip weals above and below his eyes, Bowman by his neatly pointed beard which jutted from his strong jaw. Both were rangy, rawboned, extremely tall men with whipcord muscles that warned of speed and power. They shared the same hatred of the lawless element in society. Each had suffered personal loss and vowed to seek out and, if necessary, gun down the evil men who preyed on their fellows.

On one of the stools sat Alf Pugh, the Lewis telegraph manager. He wore wire-rimmed spectacles, his hair was neatly cut and white as snow, and he exuded an air of well scrubbed good health.

Brack Bowman smiled at him gratefully. "Thanks, Alf. 'Preciate you bringin' that wire so prompt."

Alf chuckled, "Shucks young feller, we're only next door! Wasn't worth saddlin' my hoss!"

"You got a hoss? Didn't know we bred 'em that big," the deputy teased, eyeing Alf's paunch.

Alf stood. "It's gettin' kinda late, Brack. So if'n you got any notion o' sendin' replies, do it soon! Guy like me just has to have his sleep; so make it afore midnight, eh?"

Brack reread the message from Massingham Town. It asked if he knew a Frankie Dorrell, currently calling himself Pete Towers, possibly ex-Lewis citizen.

Bowman's face was stony, then he smiled like moonlight glinting on a frozen lake.

Dorrell, the killer who'd shot Bowman's father many years ago, then lit out of Lewis as soon as he'd heard of Brack's return to town. The man he hadn't pursued because of a promise to his bride. Now she'd died in childbirth, and he was free to go after the man. Just a few days ride away!

He rose lithely, moved behind his chair and went through a door into the cell block. There were three cells built of brick without windows. One cell was occupied by a young cowhand who'd been seeking work after completing a drive. It had been a bad drive with the cattle spooked by owl-hoots and lost. For six months of hard work in all kinds of weather his pay had been almost nothing. Then he'd made a gruesome discovery which drove him straight to the Lewis lawmen's office.

The lad had been terrified that he

might be accused of the crime. He was grateful to find that the tough looking bearded deputy seemed to believe his story and had given him a cell for the night. Life could be hard on a broke 16-year-old in a strange town; a bed in a friendly cell was heaven.

Bowman shook him gently awake.

Fear broke across his face, "I told you all I know, sir — I never done it. Hell, I ain't ever fired a g-g-gun!"

Bowman's eyes softened.

"Relax, son. If'n I thought you'd done it, you'd be handcuffed an' hogtied, an' I'd have taken your clothes, an' fed you on knuckles! So you can stop shakin' a minute an' tell me once more what happened."

Relieved, the young cowhand went over his story, and all the details were the same.

A day or so east of Massingham Town, where he'd stopped a night, he'd seen a burly man on a skinny palomino. He'd heard a single shot prior to the man's appearance and, having no gun of his own, he'd pulled into a thicket. He didn't think the man had seen him, but he couldn't be sure. Ten minutes later he left the thicket very carefully. He'd no water and so he looked for a stream. While doing so, he'd seen the body. Little was left of its head ... The memory caused him to turn pale and swallow convulsively.

He'd seen a few pelts and a grulla hobbled a little way off. He watered the beast and noticed that the rifle boot it carried was empty. It had seemed odd that a man who looked like a trapper had no rifle ... He'd ridden straight to Lewis to report his grisly find.

Brack intervened, "Why didn't you ride back to Massingham Town?"

The lad put his head between his hands and breathed hard. "I worn't keen to ride back over the same ground. When I seen that murderin' hellion's tracks goin' that way, I figured if he'd seen me, my life worn't worth a

79

plugged nickel. So I rode the opposite way, sir."

Bowman was about to speak when the boy sat up again.

"I just remembered somethin', sir. There was letters burned on that boot. It said 'PT'."

When he heard those initials Bowman sat up as well. His ice-cold eyes bored into the lad. "You sure that's what you saw? The sheriff rode out that way with a coupla the boys. You woulda been taken along if'n he'd thought you had anythin' to do with it, son. You done me a real favour tellin' me 'bout them initials. I'm mighty obliged to you. Now go back to sleep."

Bowman stroked his beard thoughtfully. The sheriff would be back tomorrow with the body and the evidence.

Yes, he thought, I can send a telegraph to Sheriff Massingham an' get the murderin' bastard behind bars. He'd no doubt that the initials PT had been adopted by Frankie Dorrell after the killing. His father's murderer was within his grasp.

He went back into his office and poured a stiff drink from the whisky bottle the sheriff kept in a drawer of his desk. He gulped it down and then began to draft a telegraph to Sheriff Massingham. He wrote quickly, knowing Alf Pugh would clean it up for him. DORRELL WANTED FOR MURDER HERE. ALSO SUSPECTED RECENT KILLER OF TRAPPER, INITIALS PT. EAST OF YOU. WITNESS PLACES MAN, POSSIBLY DORRELL, AT SCENE WHEN SHOT HEARD. HOLD AT ALL COSTS. ARRIVING SOONEST. BOWMAN. DEPUTY.

He hurried next door and thrust the draft into Alf Pugh's hands.

"Can you tidy it, Alf? I reckon it says it all."

Alf regarded him owlishly; the deputy was all fired up about something, and it wasn't hard to guess what it was.

"Except p'raps you left out 'My

father's murder' before the word 'here', eh Brack?"

Bowman's face was set in granite lines. "I ain't forgettin'; it just ain't relevant whose father he killed."

He strode into the night, saddled his horse and was soon at home on the ranch he shared with his family. Once there he began packing for the journey. His mother and sister watched him in silence.

When he was ready to leave, his mother whispered a single word, "Dorrell?"

He kissed her gently, "Tell Wes when he gets in, will you?"

She nodded wordlessly.

Back at the office he paced the confined space like a caged cougar. Waiting for the sheriff to return was driving him crazy. The noise of roistering drunks in the street frayed his nerves ragged.

"Hold that damn noise down!" he roared suddenly. "Folks are entitled to their sleep."

A deathly silence fell over the town; Bowman was no man to be argued with. In his cell the young cowhand grinned drowsily. "That's what I call a lawman," he murmured, "Keepin' the whole town quiet, just for me!"

7

THE day started dull and overcast. Every so often the sun would shaft down through a wind-torn hole in the clouds which would then close up again almost immediately. Each time that happened the day seemed even darker.

Massingham eyed the sky before he threw the folded slicker over his shoulder and set out from his office to visit Roy. Although they shared the same house, Massingham was always up and out before the telegraph manager went to work.

Roy beamed at him in welcome, "Here y'are, young Massingham, wire for you. Seems they want Mr Dorrell in Lewis for a necktie party. Two charges, by the look o' it."

Massingham seized the scrap of paper, scanned it and turned to Roy.

"Seems that rifle coulda belonged to a trapper, initials PT, who got murdered."

"So, Mr Dorrell who was on the run from Lewis was hidin' over to Santa Fe. He comes back here, prob'ly to rob the bank an' kills the trapper on the way. Takes a fancy to his ole Hawken, sees the initials PT an' calls himself Pete Towers when he gets here."

Roy rubbed his chin with a faint rasp of bristle.

"Yeah, I wired Santa Fe too; they don't know no Dorrell nor Towers; so God knows what he called himself there."

Massingham smiled darkly. "The hangman won't give a shit when he slips that noose round the guy's neck. Pity he can't be hanged twice; first as Dorrell, second as Towers."

Roy poured two coffees, and handed the sheriff one. "Telegraph says the Lewis depity's comin' for Dorrell. You'll have to let him take him; it's a murder charge there so — "

Massingham's lips tightened. "OK Roy, I know. Personally, I don't give a plugged dollar which town hangs him, so long as he hangs."

Bert hurried in.

"Dorrell's packed his bag an' paid his bill. He's eatin' breakfast an' — "

Massingham cut in with a laugh, "Why thank you, Bert. What's he havin' for breakfast?"

"Three fried eggs an' toast an' — Oh shit, you're just funnin' me again, ain't you? I reckon it's drinkin' so much darned coffee makes you like that, Mass. If'n that's so, I'll stick to whisky!"

Massingham gave him the telegraph. "When you've read that you'll know as much as us; mighty interestin' readin', Bert."

Just then the telegraph machinery burst into life, buzzing and chattering. Roy moved to deal with it. When silence fell again he turned to the lawmen. "Waal, just read this boys."

86

The sheriff read aloud, TRAPPER IDENTIFIED AS PATRICK THEW. DEPUTY BOWMAN TO COLLECT PRISONER APPROX 3 P.M. SHERIFF HOWE. LEWIS.

Roy shook his head, "Three o'clock? He gonna sprout wings?"

Bert chuckled as he twirled one of his moustaches round a finger, "Dorrell won't be wantin' no map again; he ain't goin' back to Santa Fe or nowheres now." He went on to tell his companions how he'd seen a map spread on Dorrell's bed, with Santa Fe and a place called Vengo marked with crosses. "I got to get back now," he finished. "When Roy rings that bell, you still gonna need me? Or are you fixin' to keep all the fun to yourself, Mass?"

Massingham shook his head, "Wouldn't dream o' it, Bert. Come arunnin', but don't bring your gun. Y'see, I got a slight change o' plan. When he draws on us poor defenceless lawmen, I'll just have to break his blamed jaw! Then there'll be the extra charge o' attempted murder o' unarmed law officers. Can't make that stick if'n we got a gun on him, now can we?"

Bert looked at him long and hard.

"Mass, you sure got it in for that jasper, an' I'm gonna enjoy seein' you thump him after he's tried to gun us down!"

After Bert returned to the Prairie, Roy looked at Massingham soberly. "You certain 'bout them Smith & Wessons? I don't want my ole job forced back on me. Who ever heard of a sheriff on sticks, eh?"

Massingham kept a poker face. "Roy, if'n them guns work, I promise you a bottle o' the best whisky every day for a year!"

"Ha!" snorted Bert, "I ain't simple y'know. Dead men don't buy whisky!" Then his face clouded, "You sure Dorrell ain't found his own gun, the one he was huntin' all round the fence for?"

"No, he ain't. I been out an' scouted round. An' guess what? I found a bit o' twine with a gun on the end. Mind you, I had a little help. There was a dog diggin' away at it as if'n he was scratchin' up a bone!"

Roy smiled in relief, "Glad to hear 'bout that; maybe you'd better get one for the poor ole dog, eh?"

Massingham scratched his head, "What in hell would a mangy ole dog do with a gun? I ain't never seen — "

"Hell Mass! I liked you better in the ole days when you was a miserable sonofabitch! Still, seems you've fixed everythin' just fine, an' that's just as well. Don't bear thinkin' about what'd happen if'n that jasper got away with the money."

Massingham grunted sourly, "Well, let it alone then. That deputy Bowman must be darned keen. Can he really be here by three o'clock, Roy?"

Roy lashed out at a circling wasp with his stick.

"Gotcha! Yeah, he could do it if'n he was determined enough, an' I got the feelin' he's gonna ride non-stop."

"Well," the sheriff said quietly, "I gotta make sure his prisoner's behind bars in one piece. Guess I better not hit him too hard."

As he watched him duck under the door Roy smiled wryly. Massingham seemed on the surface to have mellowed, always ready to crack a joke or go in for a little teasing . . . Underneath he still burned with hatred of the sort of men who'd killed his parents and his bride-to-be. What with him, and Brack Bowman on his way, Dorrell was in for a rough ride, just as sure as the sun rose every day.

★ ★ ★

Massingham eyed the sky and wondered how soon it would rain. That deputy from Lewis would be getting a good soaking. A long, hard ride and being half drowned wasn't likely to be good for his mood.

Better put him up at our place, he

thought, an' Roy'll be glad of another lawman to talk to.

He thought about Dorrell. It wouldn't be long before he made his move and Massingham decided to go back to his office awhile, then lock up and head for Jackson's. Dorrell could easily check to see if he was there. He produced and lit a cigar, and allowed himself a satisfied smile. Surely he'd got all ends covered . . .

* * *

Roy Greensleaves pinned a note on his office door. Then he took his stick and limped down Main Street. By the Lucky Star saloon he pulled out his pocket watch, and saw that it was still only eleven o'clock. Plenty of time to see Doc Lloyd and get back to his office.

Nevertheless, he was pleased it was only a short walk. The old wound in his leg was giving him trouble. At night the pain kept him awake, and in the silence of the empty hours the memories of Rita Massingham flooded his mind. He recalled with agonizing clarity the day he'd been going to marry her, and how Slim Gaunt had murdered her and Massingham's bride-to-be in the same ambush in which he'd been crippled himself.

Yes, the nights were bad times but recently he'd started feeling tired and light-headed in the days. He'd put off visiting Doc Lloyd as long as he could, but now he just had to get something for the pain.

Doc Lloyd was a dark-haired, stocky man with spectacles and a cheery smile. He was also quiet and efficient, and always ready to give Roy plenty of time. Today was no exception; he examined the ex-sheriff from top to toe, and listened carefully to what his patient said.

When Roy had finished, he gave his diagnosis.

"You're a mite short on blood, Roy, an' just tuckered out with the pain and no sleep. I'm going to give you something for the pain. You take the pills at night, get some sleep and we'll sort out the blood problem in a day or so."

He poured a dark liquid into a whisky glass and ordered Roy to drink it in one go. "Tastes awful," he said, "But it'll help almost at once."

Roy drank the stuff, and shuddered. "Hope it does. Gotta get back to the telegraph office, Doc."

Doc Lloyd shook his head. "Your office can keep awhile. Just close your eyes, an' lie back on the couch . . ."

Roy was reluctant.

"Well, maybe just for a few minutes," he allowed. As soon as he was on the couch he felt his eyes growing heavy. In a short time he was fast asleep.

Doc Lloyd smiled at the sleeping man.

"Have you right in no time, Roy. You'll sleep like a baby 'till bedtime, then you'll get another dose!" He wrinkled his brow, "What was it

Shakespeare wrote? 'Sleep that knits up the ravelled sleeve of care. Balm of hurt minds. Chief nourisher in life's feast . . . '

"Sleep well, Roy old friend."

★ ★ ★

Shortly before midday Frankie Dorrell went to the stables, and picked out a big, sturdy chestnut with four white socks. A handsome animal that pleased the eye, a shade overweight but most of that would be shed before he disposed of it. He paid more than he'd intended, but that was all right. He'd a long ride to Vengo and then on to Santa Fe, and the trapper's money was paying for it.

Vengo.

That was where the Johnson brothers were holed up, six impoverished gunslingers who'd gun down their grandmother for a dollar. Paid with cash from the bank, they'd ride to Lewis and bury that bastard Bowman. Then there would be no more looking

94

over his shoulder.

A disconcerting thought wiped the grin from his lips. He'd have to stay in that rat-hole Vengo until they returned with proof that they'd done the job. If he paid in advance they'd likely take his money and ride off into the sunset.

"Shit!" he moaned. If ever there was a dismal hole, it was Vengo. No railroad within God knows how many days ride, no telegraph, no decent hotel.

"Oh Christ!" he muttered, "The women. Scrawny as rats, stinkin' o' gin an' sweat. Could be ten days o' pure hell!"

He'd set the Johnsons a hard task, make 'em bring him Bowman's head as proof. Kinda like John the Baptist with no goddam Salome in sight!

Under his black broadcloth coat Dorrell wore a brand new Bowie knife. He jigged the chestnut to the telegraph office and hitched it to the rail. Everything was going according to plan.

He was less than pleased to read the note pinned to the door. BACK AS SOON AS POSSIBLE. HANG ON!

Hell's bloody teeth! Satan's balls! Now he couldn't hang round inside, looking out of the window to watch for Massingham to pass. Grinding his teeth, he hunted through his pockets for a cigar, then could have whooped with joy when he saw the sheriff coming towards him. Christ, the man looked a mountain, and all of it bone and muscle. His hand twitched with a near uncontrollable urge to grab for the Bowie knife and sink it into the lawman.

He thrust both hands into his pockets and forced a smile. "Hi Sheriff. I was hopin' to send a wire to Lewis, but the blamed office is closed. I'm off to Lewis soon, but maybe I'll drop round for a beer with you in a minute. But if'n I don't make it, enjoy your meal."

Massingham nodded approval at the chestnut. "You sure bought a good-lookin' hoss, Mister."

Then he added cryptically, "But things ain't always what they seem. Well, hope it don't rain. Ridin' to Lewis, was it? Man could get well soaked."

"Rain don't worry me, Sheriff," Dorrell grunted.

Massingham turned and headed away, smiling to himself. "Damn sure the rain ain't gonna bother you, Mr Dorrell," he breathed. "Not in our cell."

Dorrell watched him stride down the main street towards the bridge, and beyond it Jackson's. "What a sucker!" he whispered.

Nevertheless, he breathed deeply several times to calm himself. It was plain that the sheriff didn't like him. When the whip marks round his eyes started to glow, it was a dead giveaway.

"What the hell?" he told himself. "I sure don't like him either."

Martha Evans was stomping round the corner and Dorrell almost ran into her. He scowled, then swept off his hat and bowed mockingly.

"Stupid ole bitch," he muttered when she'd passed, "How could any man think of gettin' it up there, let alone reach the point of leavin' her at the altar?" He hung around a few minutes fiddling with the chestnut's girths to give the sheriff time to reach Jackson's.

If he'd seen Massingham's sunny smile he would have felt distinctly uneasy. The sheriff didn't see how things could be better. Even if Dorrell hit the bank and got clean away with the money, he'd still be in trouble up to his neck.

The beautiful chestnut was nicknamed 'Old Forty' by the stable. The horse had a special quirk which was all his own. Forty miles was his limit; he'd bowl along merrily until the clock in his head told him that he'd covered forty miles. No matter how many stops on the way, forty miles was his time to rest. No power on earth would move him until he'd rested at least half a day.

He'd defied the best experts in the business. The thing was imprinted on his brain, and that was that. At least half a dozen times furious buyers had returned the horse, and there had been one or two real ruckuses. Massingham's mind danced happily round the picture of Dorrell getting away. Dorrell sitting in a downpour forty miles off, fuming helplessly as he waited for the lawmen to catch up with him.

He shook his head, smiling soberly. Dorrell had to be sitting in that jail when Bowman arrived from Lewis. The deputy was likely to be wet himself; he wouldn't want to go chasing all over the county . . .

★ ★ ★

Dorrell sauntered to the sheriff's office. Not a soul in sight; the chill breeze was keeping the bastards out of his hair. But those clouds . . . "Well, if'n I get a little wettin', ain't gonna be too bad," he muttered, "Better a rich, wet man than a poor, dry one any day!"

A roaming dog loped ahead to the office door. There it lifted a leg and did a good long stream before trotting on its way.

"That's 'zactly how I feel 'bout that sheriff, ole boy!" he chuckled as he slipped a small tube of metal under the hasp of the lock.

In a moment he was inside.

Panic slapped at him as he saw the empty desk. Where the hell were the guns? His heart hammered at his ribs and he could feel his nails digging into the palms of his hands. "Shit! Shit! Shit!" he spat.

It was a trick Massingham hadn't been able to resist. He'd almost been able to feel what the man's reaction would be when he couldn't see the guns where they were meant to be.

With a gasp of relief Dorrell saw them hanging over a chair in a shadow filled corner. He snatched the guns from the holsters and thrust them into his belt under his long coat. As he left he closed the door carefully.

"Easy as takin' candy from a baby!" he rejoiced aloud. "What a shitlickin' town, with a real dumb asshole for a sheriff. A real big asshole!"

Whistling, he collected his bag from the chestnut waiting patiently outside the telegraph office. Careful to heft the bag to make it look heavy, he walked the short distance to the bank.

It was empty save for the tall bespectacled manager.

Monty Upton was reading a book on the English theatre, and wishing he was back on the stage. However, he looked forward to his forthcoming encounter with a bank robber armed with useless guns!

Bert had promised him he would be safe, but had extracted a promise from Monty that he would not put the man on guard by being too calm and unruffled. When Monty said he would put on a real act for the gunman, Bert said firmly, "Now look here Monty, don't go hamming it up, he might smell a rat, just act kinda naturally, a bit worried, frightened even, but not terrified, eh?"

Reluctantly Monty agreed — he had rather liked the idea of putting on a big act.

Putting his book aside, he glanced at the wall clock and sighed. "Come on mister, get the show on the road." He jumped involuntarily as the wish was granted. The door swung open and he found himself looking down the wrong end of a well oiled and deadly looking weapon. The man behind it was burly and mean looking, the sort that Sheriff Massingham delighted in dealing with. He repressed a shiver, Bert had promised him the gun wouldn't hurt anyone, hadn't he?

He smiled inwardly and then affected a slight stutter, "C-can I help you sir?"

"Sure, just fill this bag, and I don't want no dimes, not unless you're tired o' life friend," Dorrell grated.

Monty felt an involuntary shake in

his hands as he replied stiffly, "I most certainly am n-not tired of life, sir, I'm too young to die."

Dorrell's eyes smoked. "You ain't *that* young, friend, you ain't gonna see fifty again, won't see your next birthday if you don't fill this bag pronto." He waggled the gun and pulled back the hammer. "Mind you, I might just plug you for the hell o' it!"

Then Monty felt affronted, and opened his mouth and put his foot in it. "With due respect, sir, I'd advise against firing that gun unnecessarily, or Sheriff Massingham will come running with his deputy and half the town. You can't shoot them all, s–sir."

"Well thanks, friend," Dorrell said quietly. Then he gritted savagely as he waved the Bowie knife under the unfortunate manager's nose, "Now get on with it, pronto pronto!"

The fun fled from the day for Monty. That knife was real, deadly, menacingly real. He complied with the man's orders with alacrity, even adding ten dollars from his own wallet.

The bag was soon filled, but Dorrell's greed made him run his eye over Monty's hands. "That there gold ring you're wearin', gimme, hand it over."

Monty had no need to use histrionics, that knife looked sharp enough to hack the ring from his finger.

"Please s-sir, be reasonable, that's my mother's wedding-ring, I've given you m-more money than you can spend in ten years."

Dorrell snatched the ring from Monty's fingers, "Damn your ma. Remember now, if you set up a hollerin' when I leave, I'll come back to part your Adam's apple from your throat, right?"

Monty believed him. In an effort to placate the man he stuffed his silk handkerchief into his own mouth and sat with his hands on his head. Dorrell hefted the bag and glanced down at the bank manager with scorn. "Ain't you a goddam hero? Shoulda made you sheriff of this one-eyed town."

He left the bank and sprinted to

where the handsome chestnut awaited him. Sure was the craziest town he'd ever seen, Dorrell reflected, a dumb ox sheriff, a crazy old bitch, all of 'em, crazy everyone.

As he swung into the saddle he glanced at the sky. It didn't please him. Thunderheads were building in the east, thick and heavy looking, purplish-grey in colour and promising misery.

He leaned forward and whispered in the horse's ear, "If'n I had time, I'd of looked out that old bitch and given her a kiss, maybe I'll come back eh?" The horse snorted and tossed his head.

"You don't believe me eh? Well, you ain't so dumb as you look!"

The chestnut's stride was easy as he rode down main street and past the gatehouse. "Keep the ole rifle," he yelled as he spurred the horse to a gallop.

"What a flier!" he chuckled, "I sure can pick 'em!"

The question was, how long would the horse go on flying? . . .

8

MASSINGHAM propped up the bar in Jackson's and relished a cigar and beer.

He glanced at the clock over the barman's head. Half past twelve. Right now Dorrell would be making his move. He sank his beer, stuck the cigar between his lips and left the saloon.

As he always did, he paused on the little bridge to look at the water. Where it flowed slowly rain spots were pitting the surface.

"Poor ole Bowman's gonna get wet soon if'n he ain't already," he informed a small brown bird watching him suspiciously from along the bridge rail. An oppressive silence gripped the town. His hat banded his brow tightly and he could feel sweat trickling beneath his shirt. The air was oven-hot and breathing was difficult.

All at once a dog howled dismally, and was echoed by dozens of others.

"Thank God for that," Massingham said to himself, "I was startin' to think I'd gone deaf an' couldn't hear the blamed bell."

Nevertheless, he couldn't shake off a feeling of impending doom. It was now a quarter to one.

Unless Dorrell was wholly incompetent, the bank should have been robbed in the last ten minutes. Massingham told himself to stop worrying; force a smile, count to ten. No, make it twenty, and sure as hell he'd hear the bell. He counted to thirty. With fear curdling his stomach, he quickened his pace.

Phil Joyner, the mayor and owner of the largest general store in town, was walking towards him.

His face split with grin, "Hi, Mass. Ain't seen your pardner, have you?"

"Bert? No, why?"

"Not Bert. No doubt he's busy

somewhere, more'n can be said for Roy."

Massingham's fear grew, moved up from his stomach and took him by the throat.

"Roy? What you talkin' 'bout, Phil?"

Phil Joyner noted his anxiety. "Nothin' to get excited about, son. I tried to send a wire about an hour ago, but he worn't in. Still ain't in. Prob'ly jawin' somewheres — "

He stood and gaped as Massingham took off at a run.

"Ain't that urgent. I can wait awhiles," he finished lamely.

He shook his head and went on his way; the sheriff was a law to himself. Still, what he did suited the mayor well enough. Odd though, the way he'd run off . . . Phil Joyner made a mental note to ask him about it sometime.

The sheriff's long legs ate up the distance to the telegraph office. Reading the note on the door, he dashed to the bank.

Monty Upton greeted him with a wry smile.

"I'm afraid he's got the money."

Massingham groaned, and chewed at his knuckles.

Monty's brow creased. "But that was what you wanted, wasn't it? Presumably you've got him in jail. I'd like to have seen him get his comeuppance!"

Massingham blushed. "He ain't in jail; due to a slight hitch I never even seen him."

Monty Upton's face turned the colour of old paper. "A slight hitch? Slight hitch? Man gets away with close on thirty thousand dollars, and you talk of a *slight hitch*?!"

Massingham looked as if he couldn't believe his own words.

"Roy's disappeared; should've rung the bell. But he's just disappeared!"

Monty settled his hornrims upon his nose, and peered closely at the sheriff. The young lawman was the very picture of misery, and Monty's anger subsided.

"Best laid plans and all that," he murmured, "But maybe you'd better get rolling drunk. People have notoriously short memories where their money's concerned. Some will say you connived at the robbery and, as they say in these parts, they'll 'nail your hide to the barn door' when they find out you baited *your* trap with *their* money."

Massingham shook his head ruefully, "Thanks, Monty. I feel a whole heap better now!"

A peal of thunder rolled over the town, and they heard dogs howl at it. Abruptly, rain sheeted down as if the sky was a lake which had suddenly ruptured. In moments the dusty streets became muddy, then a quagmire.

"How long's that jasper been gone, Monty?" Massingham shouted through the roar of the rain.

"I should guess about forty to fifty minutes, but when you're as afraid as I was, time hangs a little heavily."

The sheriff stood in the doorway and watched the storm hammer the town.

A similar storm would break round his head when the townsfolk heard of what had happened. Thunder exploded almost over his head and a brilliant flash of lightning forked to the ground at the same instant. The pounding rain was a thick curtain which blotted out buildings less than twenty yards off.

Massingham groaned. "Where in hell's Roy? He's gotten me in a heap o' trouble an' no mistake."

A voice spoke behind him. "Nope, you dropped yourself in it with this harebrained scheme o' your'n, Mass. Wantin' to charge Dorrell with just 'bout every dam thing's took over from your brains. Plain loco."

Massingham glared at his sopping deputy. "Thanks for your vote o' confidence, Bert. Nice to know I got a real friend here; feller I can always count on."

"Mass, I'd stand in hell alongside o' you, an' you know it. I'd trust you anywheres, but you gotta agree we both fouled up here, me as much

111

as you. Shoulda got someone else to ring the bell, an' I should've blocked the way outa town, just in case."

Massingham nodded. "Yep. Or p'raps I shoulda acted on what we got from Lewis, just arrested the bastard an' let that depity cart him off to the hangman."

The bank manager shook his head sadly, "Isn't hindsight a wonderful thing, gentlemen? Don't blame your-selves. No one got hurt, although I was scared half to death. By the way," he added, "I saw Roy this morning. He said he was going to slip out to see the doctor."

He fixed them with a businesslike stare. "The question is what you propose to do about this unfortunate, er, contretemps. How long will it take you to catch up with the bank's money?" He cleared his throat and added, not quite able to keep a hint of reproach from his voice, "And my gold ring?"

Massingham bit off the end of a cigar.

He stuck it between his lips and told the bank manager grimly, "'Bout as long's it takes him to cover forty miles. He's riding dear ole Forty, an' he ain't gonna be ridin' fast in this weather. So pretty dam soon he'll be hunkered down in the mud somewheres an' cursin' the hoss!"

Bert pulled off his shirt. To the bank manager's disgust, he began to wring it onto the polished floor.

"We better wire Slade, Tarnville, Yellowsnake an' Vengo. No use takin' chances, eh, Mass?"

"Vengo can't be done. No telegraph there," offered the banker.

Massingham gave Bert a level stare. "Sorry to ask you to get wet again, but you better roust out Roy from the doc's. God knows what's keepin' him all this time. Have him wire everywhere Dorrell might go, though it's pretty damn sure he'll go straight to Vengo, from what you saw on that map."

Bert grunted. "If'n that damn hoss decides to change his nature, we're gonna have a long ride to Vengo. He's got a big start on us. Mass, I'm frozen through, an' you want me to go out there — "

A grin quirked up the corners of Massingham's mouth, "Look on the bright side, pardner. You can't get any wetter!"

Bert slapped on his hat and moved out into the storm. "That depity Bowman'll be double happy when he gets here," he called back, flinching at the impact of the rain, "Half drowned, tuckered out an' starvin' hungry, an' his prisoner gone!"

Massingham exchanged glances with the banker. "Ain't exactly ecstatic ourselves, are we Monty?"

Monty smiled wrily. "That's for sure. When do you propose to start your pursuit?"

"When that depity's here an' rested. No point chasin' off this very minute, specially if'n that guy's ridin' ole Forty. Always knew that hoss'd be useful one o' these days!"

Monty opened a drawer of his desk and took out a bottle of whisky. He poured Massingham a generous drink.

"Drink up, Sheriff. Don't look so gloomy; he didn't get *all* the money. If you want me to keep quiet about this a few days, I can do."

"Thanks, Monty," the sheriff breathed. "Be mighty obliged if'n you could. I don't wanna look as big a fool as I feel."

Monty blushed and paid careful attention to polishing his glasses. "Sheriff, it's the least I can do for a town that's been good to me. But just make sure I get my ring back."

Then he let out a snort of laughter, "I was going to ham it up, but the way he looked . . . Suddenly I really was terrified. You should have been there!"

The sheriff was in no mood to laugh. He smiled tightly; then his face set in hard lines.

"Shit 'n' hellfire!" he muttered.

"Something wrong, Sheriff?" Monty enquired.

Massingham pointed down the street and gave vent to a heavy sigh.

"That depity. Musta rode like the devil himself. An' he don't look none too happy. When I tell him his prisoner's gone, I reckon he's gonna be even less amused."

He shook his head dispiritedly.

If he'd known that the man called Dorrell had murdered Bowman's father, he'd have been even more unhappy.

9

THE rain stopped as suddenly as it had begun and once again hot sunlight shafted through the clouds. As they tore into tatters and streamers, the town steamed with sun-gold mist.

Brack Bowman slithered from his saddle and hitched his buckskin outside the sheriff's office. As he looked up Massingham was approaching.

He inclined his head towards the door.

"Someone's busted your lock. Ain't you got no law round here?" he teased.

"You look like a man needin' hot coffee 'n' whisky, are you Bowman?"

Brack pointed at his badge, "Yeah, an' my hardware's at your gatehouse. Man feels kinda naked when his guns've been took off'n him," he growled.

Massingham nodded sympathetically,

"Yeah, but look on the bright side, Bowman. Ain't no one gonna shoot you, and you sure look big enough to take care o' yourself if'n anyone gets fractious."

Like Massingham, Bowman had to stoop his head as he followed the sheriff into his office. Massingham waved him into a chair, removed a bottle of whisky from a drawer of his desk and poured a generous measure into a small glass. Then he strode to a cupboard and produced a couple of blankets. "We'd best get rubbed down afore we die of pneumonia," he grunted, "How far did you ride through that storm, Bowman?"

The deputy swallowed the amber liquid, and let out a contented sigh as warmth returned to his limbs.

"Name's Brack . . . You're — "

"Massingham. Always been just that since I was a kid. Pa was Massingham One an' I was Massingham Two."

Brack smiled, "OK Massingham. Tried like hell to keep ahead o' this blamed storm; it was like tryin' to outrun an express train. Can't be done."

He held out his glass and the sheriff poured him another stiff measure, then handed him the blanket. They downed their whisky in silence, and the lines slowly eased from Bowman's face as warmth crept into his limbs. Nevertheless, something was scratching at his mind, a feeling he couldn't pin down that all was not well.

"I want a good look at Dorrell. Waited a long time for this. Where d'you keep the prisoners, Massingham?"

The sheriff felt his stomach knit up tightly. He pointed to a solid oak door that looked as if it had been carved from the keel of a galleon, and took a deep breath. "Cells are through there, Brack, but we ain't got no prisoners in 'em."

Bowman's eyes were stony. "Not one? You ain't *killed* Mr Back-shootin' Dorrell? Please say — "

Massingham felt even more sick, but

he wondered why Bowman was so all-fired up about this particular killer. In his view, one rat was much the same as another.

He shook his head, "Nope, Brack, he's alive. Vamoosed just before the storm broke, but you wanna hear somethin' that'll make you feel a mite better? He's ridin' a hoss that won't budge after forty mile. Not till he's good 'n' ready. So — "

Brack Bowman came out of his chair. His teeth were audibly grinding and his hands were balled into fists.

"Escaped?" he hissed. "You let him get away? What kinda sheriff are you? I'm gonna take your head off! You useless son — "

A voice from the doorway cut him off. Ex-Sheriff Greensleaves stood there, leaning heavily on his stick.

"I ain't pushed through all this damn mud to watch a sheriff an' a depity fight! Dorrell will get clean away if'n you two half kill each other. So sit down both o' you!"

120

Roy's voice carried a ring of authority. The two men sat down reluctantly. Massingham shot his friend a warning glance. Keep your mouth shut, for God's sake; no need to tell this guy about this mess, leastways not all of it . . .

Roy pointed across the street at the telegraph office which was steaming in the sun. "Hope no one needed me. Got held up at the doc's."

"Brack, I'm sorry your prisoner got away," Massingham said earnestly, "Specially as he was wanted not just for murder in Lewis but for the suspected killin' o' that trapper. But — "

"But nothin'!" Brack snapped. You don't know the half o' it, Sheriff. I want that feller so much I'm bustin' a gut! As far's you're concerned, he ain't done nothin' here."

"Wrong! He smuggled in a gun an' robbed the bank! I never knew nothin' until he'd gone," countered Massingham sharply.

Roy simply went on leaning on his stick and gazed at the ceiling, as if the pattern of cracks in it was of intense interest. It was clear to him that Massingham didn't want Bowman to know about the farce of Dorrell's escape, and who could wonder at it? He'd make sure that, as far as he was able to ensure it, the sheriff wouldn't be further embarrassed.

Brack relaxed slightly, "So you've got a reason to go after him. Well just remember that I got *first* call on him. An' I don't aim to waste the judge's time, nor the hangman's either, if'n I can help it!"

The sheriff's eyes turned into grey pools of ice. "I'm a lawman, not an executioner. He'll face trial an', if'n they convict him, then he'll do the rope dance."

Roy intervened quickly, "OK, fellers, first catch your man, eh? Ain't no point arguin' like a coupla dogs over a bone when there ain't no bone. By the way, wires's down most everywhere, so I can't send no messages."

Massingham's eyes locked with Brack's.

"Well, maybe it don't make much difference," he said musingly. "Dorrell won't know that. He'll just push on, leastways as far as that darned hoss'll allow."

Bowman's smile was wolfish, "Fine, I don't want no one catchin' up with him afore I do. Where in hell he's gone to is what I want to know, an' do we have any good trackers here?"

"No need, we know he's headed for Vengo. I reckon he knows there ain't ever been a wire in Vengo, so he'll feel safe."

He told the bearded deputy what Bert had discovered. "Y'see, Brack," he concluded, allowing himself a smile, "We know where he's headed, an' ole Forty's on our side. So I guess we can relax."

Bowman was watching him coldly. "I still don't get what happened here.

You got my wire, so you knew he was wanted for two murders. Then you sit around while he robs your bank an' scoots with the money!"

He appealed angrily to Roy Greensleeves.

"What sorta law do you have in this town? Seems what I've heard about it's all bullshit!"

Massingham cut in at once, "What happened here ain't none o' your business. It happened, an' that's it. I'm comin' with you to get him. You can get a coupla hours sleep at my place if'n you want."

"No thanks. I'll hunker down in one o' your *empty* cells, no more'n three hours. We'll get off before dark. Take care o' my hoss, can you?"

Without another word he went through the door to the cells. Massingham and Roy heard the door of a cell open and shut. Then there was silence.

Massingham regarded Roy moodily. "He's sure got a burr under his saddle 'bout somethin' pretty important, leastways to him."

The ex-sheriff nodded thoughtfully, "Yeah, son, you're right. I guess you don't want no one talkin' 'bout what really happened. Shall I warn Bert an' Monty an' our esteemed gunsmith? Oh yeah, an' dear ole Martha. We can pretend Dorrell really did smuggle a gun into town, makes no difference. I'll keep 'em quiet if'n I have to get the doc to sew their lips together!"

Massingham smiled gratefully, "Thanks Roy, much appreciated. Guess I must look the biggest fool to ever wear a star."

Roy chuckled drily, "I done it regular when I was wearin' that badge, son. You just made your first mistake, is all."

"You never made a mess like this Roy." Massingham mopped his face with his bandanna, "This is regular humdinger. Plain stupid."

"Well, son. Just get Bowman his prisoner, and Monty his money; then no one'll be any wiser."

The sheriff shook his head, "Frankie Dorrell is gonna open his big mouth an' — "

"Then it'd be better if'n he came back *dead*," Roy retorted. "Seein' that depity's awful like lookin' at you a few years back. He's burnin' up inside. I'd say Dorrell's got as much chance of savin' his skin as Martha's got o' marryin' you!" He hesitated, and cleared his throat apologetically. "By the way, Doc Lloyd gave me somethin' that knocked me out cold. Real sorry I let you down!"

Massingham smiled gently, "You ain't never let anyone down in your life. I should've arrested Dorrell soon's we got that wire from Lewis. Stupid, just plain stupid!"

★ ★ ★

By late afternoon the sun had baked the mud like a pie crust. With sweat trickling beneath his shirt, Massingham, aided by Bert, had almost completed

126

preparations for the pursuit. As usual, the deputy's face was deeply creased with worry lines.

"Mass," he said, his anxiety showing in his voice as well, "You ain't gonna let that sun fool you, right? Y'know what happens this time o' year. Storm goes round in a damn great circle. You could get drenched again. If'n you take my advice — "

Massingham held up a hand reassuringly, "OK, Mother Hen! I've packed tarps an' slickers, along with 'bout enough stuff to feed an army. What I'd be grateful for you to do is look after the town as usual, hold back the urge to kick Doc Lloyd's ass, an' keep quiet 'bout what really happened. 'Fraid you'll have to take a few days off from the Prairie." He tipped his hat back on his head and studied their work. "Reckon that's about it?"

Bert twirled a moustache point round a finger.

"Looks that way. You gotta pick up your rifle from the gatehouse, plenty o' shells an' Bowman's hardware. Yeah, plenty o' shells."

"You pokin' fun at my shootin'?" Massingham asked, poker-faced. "Why, at the last Carnival shoot — "

"OK Mass, you beat me. Don't rub it in! Should be a law against that damn ole Hawken o' your'n."

Brack Bowman had entered the office quietly. He stood with his arms folded, and his neatly bearded chin jutted pugnaciously.

"You gonna stand round here jaw-waggin' all afternoon?"

Bert stared at him. "Talkin' 'bout jaws, Mister, you seem awful keen to get yours broke! Good for you that you're hidin' behind that badge, or our sheriff would've taught you some manners by now."

A long silence simmered in the air between them.

Then Brack held out his hand.

"Sorry fellers," he said gruffly, "But all I can think of is Frankie Dorrell. It ain't your fault. I don't usually act like a hung-over bear." A spasm of pain crossed his face. "My second wife died a coupla weeks ago. It left me free to go after Dorrell. Y'see, I got an ole score to settle with him. When I heard he was here where a famous sheriff could get him under lock an' key, I was pretty pleased. Now I find he's moved on again. Sorry I took it out on you."

The lawmen shook.

Bert asked innocently, "So you got somethin' personal with Dorrell?"

Brack's face set in granite lines, "Yeah, very personal. He killed — "

Massingham's voice was edged with iron. "It don't matter who he killed. We're bringin' him in alive!"

With arms folded, they stood and glared at each other.

Then, as electricity seemed to sizzle between them, Bert intervened. "Shit, fellers! It ain't worth arguin' 'bout; leave it in God's hands, huh?"

Massingham smiled. "Well, I'm darned, my depity's gone religious. Don't let us come back an' find

129

you switched your badge for a pulpit, ole son!"

He turned to Brack with an eye that now twinkled, and nodded at a pile of assorted clothing on a chair. "Change of duds if'n you want it. Fresh hosses, two each, saddled an' loaded. We can hit the trail when you've had some chow. See, while you was sleepin' we didn't spend all our time waggin' our jaws!"

Brack stroked his beard and grinned at the sheriff. "Reckon you ain't so bad when folks gets to know you, Massingham."

★ ★ ★

Twenty minutes later they arrived at the gatehouse where old Tom fussed like a mother hen. He trotted outside and strapped a booted rifle on Massingham's buckskin. "There y'are Sheriff, your ole gun, an' damn heavy it is!"

Massingham grinned tightly. His .60 Hawken might be heavy but he prized it for its long range.

Brack favoured a Winchester and a pearl-handled Colt.

As Tom bent down behind his counter, Massingham laughed. "Thanks ole timer. Now don't go hittin' your head on that blamed bell; it's like to get cracked clear in half!"

"Like some other folk round here," muttered Tom as he handed Brack a sheathed Army knife. "Need this?" he enquired, "Bert put a bullet through some guy who was makin' trouble with it; Massingham's got one already."

Brack accepted the weapon gratefully, "Never know when it'll come in handy. Thank you, sir."

Tom swelled visibly. "Hear that, young Massingham? This feller knows how to treat a man. When did you ever call me 'sir', eh?"

The lawmen forked their horses into a canter away from the gatehouse. Through a plume of dust, Massingham called back over his shoulder, "So long, Sir Thomas! That suit you, you cantankerous ole cuss?"

10

SOME five miles out of town Massingham reined up his buckskin.

"Look at that, Brack," he said, leaning out of his saddle and pointing at the ground, "Ole Forty's prints for sure. We ain't far wrong."

Brack drew alongside and gazed at the sun-baked mud. "That's a relief. Coupla days' ride to Vengo without a sign o' him 'ud drive me plumb loco."

Massingham passed over a cigar and they lit up.

"Gonna tell me why that jasper means so much to you? You can't feel this way 'bout every murderin' hellion who crosses your path? You'd have gone crazy long ago if'n you did."

Brack regarded the glowing tip of his

cigar. He sucked in a deep lungful of smoke, let it out and nodded. "Guess you're right. I've hunted dozens o' them, killed most. It started when one o' 'em got me sent to jail by mistake. Served a lotta time 'fore I got pardoned."

His face was set in bitter lines. "Wife took her life afore I got out, she was so 'shamed." He went on quickly, as if the words tasted bad, "My pa was killed by a back-shootin' sonofabitch an' left me a lotta money. So I spent a lotta time lookin' for fellers like him, evened things up a mite for those as couldn't defend theirselves."

His lowered voice dripped venom, "Then I got 'gaged to the judge's daughter in Lewis, at the same time I found out who murdered my daddy. He ducked outa Lewis soon's I arrived. When I married, my wife begged me to quit huntin' the bastard. She died givin' birth an' I was free to go after him. Then I got Roy's wire askin' 'bout him, so here I am . . . "

Massingham nodded. "Frankie Dorrell, huh?"

"You got it, pardner!"

Massingham studied the other man's face. He blew a smoke ring and watched it drift and fall apart. "So you lost two wives? Hell, that's three we lost between us, Brack."

"Hell of a life, ain't it?" the deputy replied shortly. "Let's get goin'."

As they trotted along a well defined trail through clumps of mesquite, Massingham's thoughts were sombre. The bones of hundreds of cattle testified that the route had been popular at one time.

He brooded about what a fool he'd been to let Dorrell escape, and poor old Brack desperately seeking his father's killer. No wonder the man had almost exploded when he'd discovered that the bird had flown . . .

As sunset was staining the western sky they arrived at what should have been the banks of a shallow river. Massingham leapt from his saddle with a snarl of frustration.

"Shit! Dorrell's crossed here, y'can see ole Forty's prints real plain. Now look at that damn flood water! Too fast, we're gonna have to bed down for the night, give the water time to slow."

Brack glowered across the river into the gloom. "Devil looks after his own, eh? Sonofabitch got across afore it rose."

They watered and hobbled their horses before rolling into their tarps, each lost in his own thoughts. If no more rain swelled the flow, with a bit of luck the level would fall before daybreak. Otherwise they'd face a time-wasting detour.

To Massingham it seemed that he'd only just fallen asleep when Brack's hand shook him awake. "Massingham!" the deputy hissed, "Water's down, c'mon, feller. Coffee's on, ham's near ready. Let's get at it afore the sun burns your eyeballs out."

Massingham rubbed gritted eyes and

yawned, "Sun? Hell, it's still dark! How long we been asleep?"

"Near five hours! Ain't a growin' boy, are you?"

Massingham rolled from his tarp and joined Brack at the fireside. His teeth showed in a grin. "Nope, finished growin'. Roy says cigars've stunted me, an' he's right 'bout most things!"

Brack gulped coffee. "You two seem pretty close. You took over from him when he retired, that right?"

When Massingham replied there was a catch in his voice.

"Slim Gaunt murdered my mother on her way to marry Roy; he murdered my gal at the same time. We was all gettin' married at the same time at Grainville, an' Gaunt crippled Roy in that ambush. So I took over. We live together an' he's like a father to me."

Brack absorbed this, and then growled, "Seems you an' me've had a rough ride. When we got Dorrell, you wanta go after this Gaunt hombre?"

Massingham's smile by way of reply

gave Brack a start; the weals round the sheriff's eyes glowed hotly in contrast to his stony eyes.

"Blew his brains away with that ole Hawken o' mine. Thanks all the same, pal."

As they forded the water, the sun rose like a hot scarlet ball over a range of hills on the horizon. It spread level rays across the land and old Forty's tracks, following the river, momentarily seemed to be splashed in blood. Massingham commented that a steady pace to allow for the horse's quirk would probably bring them to Vengo right on the heels of their quarry.

At midday the sun was a fiery orb which seemed to be scrambling their brains. They stopped to soak their bandannas in the river, then put the wet cloth inside their hats. Water trickled into their eyes and ears and steamed on their faces.

Brack sank onto a rock. He rolled a couple of quirlies and tossed one to Massingham who was watering the horses.

"Right outa cigars. Have one o' these, Mass."

With pleasure the sheriff noted Brack's use of Bert's habit of shortening his name.

He caught the smoke, lit it and inhaled luxuriously. As he did so, Brack was putting his Bull Durham on the rock behind him.

Massingham's smile froze as his gut knotted up tight. He forced his muscles to loosen into the posture of a fast gunfighter.

His voice came from between his teeth in a soft hiss, "Keep real still, Brack. If'n you so much as breathe, you ain't gonna see Dorrell."

In a blur of speed the Adams leapt into his fist, leaving his tied-down holster as if by magic.

The roar of the gunshot was echoing across the land as he smiled crookedly at Brack. "OK, buddy, relax. Another rattler bites dirt, huh?"

Brack rubbed his wrist; it was still hot from the passage of the slug. His eyes widened at the sight of a headless rattler twisting in its death throes on the rock next to his Bull Durham.

"Jesus Christ!" he blurted admiringly, "Never seen a draw like that anywhere, Mass. Reckon I owe you."

Massingham grinned sheepishly as he holstered the Adams. "Tell the truth, that was a mite faster'n I usually slap leather, less'n there's a feller drawin' on me." He took a drag on his smoke. "Well, I didn't like the thought o' havin' to get you fixed. That sonofabitch coulda got clear away with Monty's money!"

They smoked their quirlies in companionable silence. Grinding his butt under his heel, Massingham looked at the other man keenly.

"You told me why you want Dorrell, an' I think it's time I squared with you. I can count on you to keep it quiet 'cause you owe me."

Brack answered reproachfully, "You

coulda relied on me — "

Massingham laughed hollowly, "Wait 'till I've told you. It's the darnedest thing you ever heard. You're lookin' at the biggest fool as ever let a town pin a star on him."

When he finished his story, Brack shook with laughter. It went on bursting out of him until his horse pricked up its ears and stared at him, then whickered as if joining in the fun.

"Jeez, Mass," he got out at last, "Ain't never heard anythin' like that. You sure made a hog's-ear o' that. Don't tell me you made it up, don't spoil it. I gotta believe it, every word o' it!"

The sheriff shook his head ruefully, "You can believe it. Just keep it quiet, eh?"

Brack slapped Massingham on the back and chortled in delight. "Sure Mass, but who was it said 'the way to hell is paved with good intentions'? I won't say a word to no one but I can't speak for my hoss. He was mighty took with your story! We ain't never enjoyed hearin' anythin' so much!"

Massingham assumed an air of mock sorrow. "Thanks, Brack. Sure glad I gave you an' your critter some pleasure in your bleak an' miserable lives. But I ain't never heard a depity encourage his hoss to laugh at a sheriff."

★ ★ ★

Whilst Frankie Dorrell was aware that Sheriff Massingham, probably with a posse, would be on his trail, he didn't know that the man he feared and wanted dead, Brack Bowman, was also after him.

Unlike his pursuers, he had no cause for laughter. Old Forty was taking a rest, and nothing would move him. Dorrell had kicked and whipped him, twisted his tail savagely and nearly got his head kicked off in return. Now he was yelling himself hoarse, and soon would be pleading with the creature. For all the effect it was having, he might as well have sought to move one of the lightning-blasted trees that dotted the area.

He took a break, sitting down and cursing long and hard. Five hours he'd been waiting with this accursed horse. "Bloody idle bastard," he fumed. "Nothin' wrong with you 'cept sheer sonofabitchin' cussedness."

The thought that the sheriff might ride up at any moment was making his blood run first hot, then cold. He wondered bitterly if maybe the bastard horse was deaf.

He jabbed a Smith and Wesson close to Old Forty's ear. Grinning evilly, he cocked the hammer. The gun clicked, and then again.

With a howl of rage he drew its twin, and got the same result: flat clicks.

Eyebrows beetling together, he examined the weapons. At the discovery that they had been spiked, he shook his fists at the sky and screamed his frustration. "What in hell's that stinking sheriff been up to?" he shrieked, "What's he done to me?"

Dimly he perceived that a trap had been laid for him and that something had gone wrong. That old hag following him around. Had she been something to do with it?

With an effort he regained control of himself. What the hell does it matter, he thought. I've got the money. I can buy guns when I reach Vengo. *When* I get to Vengo.

If he got to Vengo. After all, he was dependent on the horse, and it wouldn't move. Damn an' blast my luck! he raged to himself. Even the goddamn hoss is against me!

He got up furiously, ready to try beating the horse again, and crowed with delight. Old Forty was standing alertly, ears pricked forward and ready to go. Whispering words of encouragement, he approached the animal cautiously. Old Forty stood and waited for him, and Dorrell gripped the saddle horn and swung himself up.

Then he urged the horse forward and Old Forty went straight into an easy canter.

A yell of triumph burst from his lips. This horse could certainly move when he wanted to. The land sloped upwards gradually away from the river, and soon he could see for miles.

No sign of pursuit.

He pushed his hat back on his head and squinted back hard along his trail. Perhaps the sheriff had lost his tracks? It seemed almost too good to be true. He'd got to reach Vengo fast. Buy some guns, hire gunslingers to ride to Lewis and kill that bloody Bowman. Then a nice, easy ride to Mexico to live like a King. All those señoritas! He was coming, he was coming!

11

THE lawmen followed the trail from the river until the great red ball of the sun sank below the horizon. The rattlesnake had shaken Brack, and he tied his tarp to a tree branch before climbing into it.

Massingham peered through the gloom. "You look like a bat! But ain't you s'posed to hang by your feet?"

"You can laugh all you like," came the muffled answer, "But I ain't trustin' to your shooting again, Mass. Felt the wind o' that shell cross my hand. Worn't no need to shoot that damn close."

Massingham chuckled as he spread out his own tarp. "You panic too easy, Brack. I threw that shell almost a quarter inch clear o' your hand!"

Soon they were both asleep. The only sounds at their campsite were the occasional soft snore, the grunting and shuffling of hobbled horses, and the far-off howls of coyotes.

Massingham's nightmare starred Monty Upton as he addressed the town council on the subject of the sheriff handing their money to Frankie Dorrell. Brack's blended rattlers and Frankie Dorrell. After only a few hours both woke unrefreshed and it was still dark when they hit the trail.

The sun heralded its arrival by shooting pink spears into the still indigo sky. Within moments the sky was blue as the golden disk swam above the eastern horizon. It was going to be an insufferably hot day for anyone travelling.

★ ★ ★

Even the most starry-eyed of Western romantics would have been forced to agree that Vengo was a dump.

A miserable conglomeration of corrugated metal shacks, it surrounded a dilapidated saloon, creaking in the heat of the afternoon sun. On the rare days when it rained, the town, streaming and red with rust, was a glimpse of purgatory. Launched by a gold strike, it had foundered when the reef was exhausted, from start to finish a matter of two years.

The people weren't much better. Those who were able to had quickly moved on. Those who couldn't and stayed cursed the weather, loafed around drinking watered-down red-eye. Gradually they'd become almost sub-human as they rubbed shoulders with outlaws on the run and awaited the odd miracle of an unsuspecting stranger stumbling into their midst.

On the blazing day Frankie Dorrell entered town they thought their prayers had been answered.

Dorrell was the only stranger they'd set eyes on in many a lean day. Like spiders crawling from their webs, the townsfolk came out of their broken-down homes to inspect him as he hitched his weary, dust-grimed mount outside the saloon. They followed him in speculative silence at a safe distance as, with his bag tucked under his arm, he lurched through the batwings and up to the counter.

He scowled at a mirror as he saw the trail dust clinging to the stubble that peppered his jowls.

The saloon-keeper was only too pleased to offer him a dingy room at the rear of the bar, and hurried to supply him with a bottle of red-eye to drink there.

When he learned in answer to his questions that the Johnson brothers had left for Wyoming over a week ago, Dorrell's face suffused with anger. Damn the lot of 'em, he thought savagely. Why waste good money to kill Bowman? Surely the bastard ain't gonna follow me to Mexico. I must be loco lettin' that ole trapper scare me. Bowman's probably suckin' pussy an' forgotten all 'bout me. Just gotta put some distance between me an' that scar-faced sonofabitchin' sheriff, that's all.

As he absentmindedly picked trail dust from his nose, he thought about his next move. Two hours rest, then hit the trail. "Oh Christ," he muttered to himself, "If'n I only knew whether that sheriff's started out yet. How far behind is he? Is he following the right trail? Oh hell, sleep's what I need." He dropped onto the lumpy bed with the grey sheets and began to gulp at the bottle. Soon he'd fallen into a stupor of exhaustion, clutching the bag with the money from the bank like a baby clinging to a cuddly toy.

In the bar three men discussed the stranger who'd held a bag so close to his chest.

One of the trio, a thin, weasel-faced man, gave his opinion in a hoarse stage whisper. "He ain't gonna be no pushover, not like that last feller. Mean lookin' hombre, an' he ain't lettin' that bag outa his sight."

A tall man with spiked red hair

snorted his derision.

"Expect him to walk up an' give it to you? Huh? It's gotta be worth our attention, but let's just give him an hour with that bottle."

The third man, who had black, greasy hair and was built like a buffalo, removed a small axe from his waistband and fingered the edge. "Nice 'n' quiet," he said nasally, "while he's sleepin' like a babe. No gunshots to wake the town. One second he's alive, the next," he drew a finger across his throat, "he ain't. Way to do it, fellers. Ain't no better, eh?"

The weasel grinned sycophantically and produced a bunch of keys from his pocket. "Yeah Cal, you got it. I'll just ease the door open an' you can bash his head straight in. No messy fightin' or bullets flyin' round." His lips peeled back in a grin, "Nobody gets hurt; even he ain't gonna feel nothin'."

The saloon-keeper was trying to stab a drunken wasp with a matchstick. He looked up at the others.

150

"Hey you guys, I don't want no mess in there. Them sheets is a bitch to get clean. Can't you just strangle him?"

The wasp lifted off and weaved away, and his thoughts followed it. Time was when a man could run a decent saloon and be proud of it, not a killing house for men who used to be good miners. He sighed deeply and leaned on the bar.

A fourth man who was as lean as whipcord and pale as sun-bleached wood came in and voiced an opinion about the disposal of the stranger. He was one of those who like to shift their ground and argue for the sake of looking knowledgeable, so the argument that ensued became heated. Loud enough to rouse Dorrell from his slumbers. With one ear to the door, the subject of the discussion wasn't lost on him.

As he quietly slid a battered cupboard against the door, he grinned wolfishly. Then he wedged the bed against it to make a tight fit across the tiny room. Grabbing his bag, he slipped out of the window and crept round to the hitching rail. He was lucky he wasn't the sort of man who took care of a horse before himself. Old Forty wasn't in a comfortable stable; he was standing patiently at the rail just waiting to go. Dorrell swung into the saddle and cursed the useless guns the sheriff had foisted upon him. It would have been such a pleasure to blow away the men who were planning his death.

The dusty road deadened the sound of the horse's hooves. As soon as he was out of town he spurred Old Forty into a gallop and a cloud of dust rose and hung in the air behind him.

In the saloon the argument went on its way.

"Where in hell's Phil Snare?" demanded the spiky redhead. "He'd slip in there 'n' slit his throat afore you could say 'Goodnight Stranger'. Can't never trust the weird sonofabitch to be here when you want him."

Weasel shivered, "Yeah, he's the meanest hombre I ever met." He looked round furtively as if Snare might pop up at any moment. "Reckon his mother was a scorpion an' his ole man a rattler. He gives me the shakes. Can't we do *nothin'* without him?"

The saloon-keeper was looking over his head past the batwings. "Lotta dust just outa town," he observed, "Wonder what all that is?"

The four men rushed from the saloon. Cal flourished his axe in rage, "You stupid bastards, he's got clear away! What a lot o' pig brained fools!" He was frothing at the lips, "Next stranger, just leave him to me an' Phil Snare. You assholes are all mouth!"

★ ★ ★

Frankie Dorrell was slumped against a tree in a small stand of pines. He was scowling at his horse which gazed back at him with total unconcern. It was another of the times when it decided it would take a rest. No matter how many short stops Dorrell gave him, Old Forty still insisted on a long break every forty miles.

He peered through the twilight, trying to make out the range of mountains on the horizon. Once beyond their peaks he'd feel safer. Up in that rocky vastness he could spy the land to pick up any pursuers. There'd also be plenty of places for an ambush. So just let that scar-faced bastard try to —

"Hell!" he spat. "Oh shit!"

With a sick feeling he recalled that he wasn't just burdened with useless handguns; he'd left the trapper's rifle and his own at the Massingham Town gatehouse. He'd aimed to buy guns in Vengo. Now he was defenceless. Somewhere, soon, he'd have to get some hardware, but where and how?

Had Brack been a vulture sitting in one of the trees, he'd have said, as he had done before, "The devil looks after his own."

Jigging a grey mare through the twilight was a young dude cowboy.

Dorrell crept behind a larger pine, and held his breath as he drew the useless guns. Although the youngster hadn't yet seen Dorrell or Old Forty, the grey threw up her head and whickered loudly.

Dorrell seized his chance.

"Hands on your head, fella!" he barked. "You're right in my sights, but I ain't gonna kill you if'n you do just as I say."

The kid's hands shot up. "I got fifty dollars you can have, mister," he cried. "You don't have to kill me."

Dorrell's grin was jubilant as he stepped into view. "Reach down real slow an' drop your gunbelt." He added menacingly, "No tricks or I'll put twelve holes in your fancy duds afore you can cry 'Help, Mother!'"

The gunbelt dropped to the ground.

"Now move your hoss away an' keep

your hands from that rifle," Dorrell growled.

The badly frightened boy complied at once.

"That far enough, mister?"

Dorrell saw that his outfit was new and he could smell the aroma of new leather boots, belt, holsters, saddle and all the other accoutrements that made up a dude cowboy. He kept his eyes glued to his victim as he bent to pick up the gunbelt.

"Yeah, far enough. Slip off'n that hoss an' get on mine after you've took my bag off. No tricks."

"Sure sir, anything you say," gabbled the youngster. "You want my fifty dollars? You're welcome."

Dorrell was enjoying himself. "Why not, friend? Always do a proper job's my motto."

The wallet dropped in front of Dorrell as the boy mounted Old Forty. "Nice hoss you got here, sir — "

"You mean nice hoss *you* got. He's all your'n now," Dorrell chuckled. He was almost bursting with glee. "Yeah friend, you're a real good judge o' hoss flesh. That there's about the most unusual hoss you'll ever come across!"

He gave the kid his gunbelt and useless revolvers.

"Here y'are. We just swopped hosses an guns! An' you gave me fifty dollars 'cause your hoss worn't so good's the one I gave you. That's what I call a real nice trade!"

The youngster was anxious to be gone before Dorrell changed his mind. "Can I go now, please, sir? It's gettin' dark an' — "

Dorrell cut across him contemptuously, "Clear off an' think yourself lucky."

Under the Mexican dude spurs Old Forty flew into the dusk at a rate that seemed to justify the bemused youngster's assessment of him.

Dorrell examined his booty with growing pleasure. Pearl-handled Colt .45s, a Winchester 1873, Model .44, and a rangy grey mare, plus fifty dollars. He picked up the wallet and counted the money. His nostrils flared.

"Thievin' little bastard! There's only forty in here. I shoulda killed him!" he snarled.

12

ON the edge of town Brack Bowman and Massingham sat their horses and smoked quirlies. The setting sun couldn't soften Vengo. In the dusky light the town was full of brooding shadows, as forbidding a place as ever they'd seen.

Their mounts picked up the atmosphere of malevolence and shifted beneath them restlessly.

Only an occasional shaft of sickly light from a doorway or window relieved the unmitigated gloom. The saloon emitted no music or laughter and a skeletal dog looked at it balefully. Then it lifted a leg on a doorpost and vanished into shadows round the side of the building.

Brack lifted himself in the saddle and scratched the back of his neck.

"Sure ain't no swanky place. Thought

this was supposed to be a boom town."

Massingham answered sombrely, "Used to be. Town's full o' deadbeats an' outlaws now. They'd kill a man for a dollar, then eat his hoss! Only boom round here's gonna be the sound o' guns if'n Dorrell's sittin' there waitin' for us."

Brack smiled tightly, "Well, Mass. He ain't gonna be expectin' me. He don't even know I'm on his trail! But I sure hope there is gonna be a boom. I don't want no palaver with judges 'n' lawyers."

The sheriff dragged smoke into his lungs and didn't reply. He didn't like the idea of rough justice, but maybe Dorrell had earned a bullet for what he'd done to Brack and his family, and sometimes a murderer preferred a bullet to dancing on the end of a rope.

They walked their horses silently into the dusty, rutted main street. Like thicker, moving shadows in the near darkness, they hitched their mounts outside the ramshackle saloon. Massingham peered over the batwings into a smoky bar lit by no more than a few candles.

"Brack, ole fella, cemetery in our town's fuller an' livelier than this place," he grunted.

Brack loosened his Peacemaker in its holster.

"Yeah, but this sorta place has a habit o' livenin' up, 'specially when lawmen ride in."

There were a dozen or so drinkers sitting over glasses of moonshine in introverted silence. The room smelled of unwashed bodies, stale tobacco and candle smoke. The drinkers regarded the lawmen speculatively. These two didn't seem the type to tangle with; a bullet in the back or a knife in the dark was a better bet. But was it worth the risk? Lawmen seldom carried much money, and killing men who wore stars always stirred a heap of trouble. An unspoken agreement in the bar kept the eyes of its denizens fixed on their drinks.

"What'll it be, gents?" the sallow barkeep asked. His eyes took in Massingham's ruined face, the ice-chip eyes . . . This was Sheriff Massingham, and the other man looked as mean, whoever he was. It would be prudent to be careful here.

Brack slapped cash on the counter. "Two beers. Can you fix us a coupla steaks?"

The barkeep smiled wanly. "For money I'd roast my granny. Money's shorter 'n summer snow round here."

Brack nodded as the man pushed their drinks across the counter. "Sorry to hear that. Seen any strangers?"

The barkeep's eyes were blank as he moved a cloth over the scarred counter. His brain worked furiously; thank Christ they hadn't killed that feller before he lit out!

Brack flipped him a coin. "Here mister. That help your deafness?"

The man attempted a grin. 'Tain't my ears, it's my memory. Can't

162

remember nothin' these days."

Massingham felt a sharp pang of sympathy. What a life, trapped and trying to do business in a hell-hole like this!

He placed a dollar on the counter. "Best medicine I know for deafness or poor memory. How 'bout answerin' questions now?"

The coin disappeared as if by magic. The man's smile was real this time. "Thank you Sheriff, thanks a lot. Big, mean-lookin' cuss rode in 'bout midday. I gave him a room in back."

Brack's eyes were dark with joy, "He there now?"

The barkeep looked down, and a shiver gripped him.

"No sir. Can't think what got into him. He, er, blocked the door, then climbed out the window. Didn't pay for his room or bottle."

Brack laid down another coin. His mouth had thinned to a white line, "That'll cover his dues. How long's he been gone?"

The man was awestruck by the money that kept appearing.

"Five hours. Hey! I recall he was askin' for some fellers, six brothers, a mean bunch o' mavericks, the Johnsons. Said he had a job for 'em over to Lewis."

The lawmen exchanged glances. Massingham punched Brack playfully. "There y'are ole son. Reckon Dorrell needed money to take care o' you."

"Sure thing Mass," Brack whispered with a grin, "An' we know whose bank gave it to him, huh?"

The barkeep was rubbing his hands eagerly, "One o' you gents say somethin' 'bout steaks?"

Massingham swigged at his drink and chuckled, "Sure, but we don't want your grilled or roasted grandmother!"

"I'm savin' her for Christmas! but let's see what we got."

Brack grunted, "If'n they're good an' come quick, you *could* get paid some more. Hurry it up, eh?"

They seated themselves at a corner

table, conscious of the covert scrutiny from every eye in the bar. Massingham stretched wearily and yawned. "Bit hard on that fella weren't you, Brack? Poor bastard's doin' his best."

"Ugh, moonshine!" Brack growled. "He'd have kept us long's he could, drinkin' his foul liquor an' spendin' dinero. The steaks would've been black an' hard as a bounty hunter's heart." He took another swig at his drink and screwed up his face. "An' all that time Dorrell woulda been gettin' further away."

The steaks came promptly and were swiftly eaten.

Brack noted the barkeep's pallor, his tired, hopeless eyes, and compassion swelled his heart.

"Best steak I've had in many a day," he said, as the man hovered, awaiting a verdict. "What say, Mass?"

The sheriff wiped his lips, "Never said a truer word, Brack. Maybe we'll call in on the way home."

The barkeep smiled ingratiatingly,

"Thanks, gents. How long afore you're back?"

Brack scowled, "Just as soon's we catch up with that hombre who jumped out your window without payin'."

Massingham kept a straight face. "Would you believe we specialize in catching jaspers that jump outa windows an' don't pay?"

Brack was impatient; he wanted Dorrell so badly it hurt. "I tell you this, mister. Sure's my name's Brack Bowman, that guy ain't gonna run out on anyone else after I've caught up with him."

The man gaped at him. You're *Brack Bowman*? I've heard 'bout you. Recall seein' your face on a flier once. Didn't you . . . "

Brack answered wearily. "Feller that looked like me. I got pardoned after breakin' half the rocks in the county."

No use, he reflected, trying to tell the story of how the man turned out to be his twin brother . . . A brother he'd never known lived, and who was now so close to him.

The man had recovered his composure. A wan smile lit his face. "Well, fancy havin' Sheriff Massingham an' Brack Bowman. Have to raise my prices for sure."

The weasel-faced man, who was sitting obscured by shadows, had a few drinks under his belt. "Well, just fancy that fellers," he said in an imitation of the barkeep's voice, "We got Bowman an' Massingham drinkin' in our humble establishment. Raise your glasses, everybody!"

The laughter which followed this was subdued; Weasel was drunk and nobody else wanted to offend these visitors.

Spiky Hair's heart trip-hammered his ribs. He could feel his shirt stick to his back and sweat trickled from his armpits. Phil Snare's brother Jed had tried a fast-gun draw on Massingham. A stone in Massingham Town cemetery was a mute testimony to the outcome of that. Spiky Hair was good and scared;

nevertheless, Phil the Knife would be pleased to know that Massingham was here.

"Another beer?" Massingham asked. "Then we'll hit the trail. Don't fancy sleepin' here, do you?"

Brack glanced round the bar. "Sooner sleep with the wolves. Some o' these characters look like they'd eat us an' our hosses, then try the saddles!"

The barkeep spoke quietly, "The wolves don't come to Vengo in winter to look for food. They're too smart. Folks'll eat anythin' they can get their hands on in this town!"

He fetched their drinks. Pretending to wipe the table top, he whispered, "Been here long 'nough to smell when somethin's in the air. I seen a feller slip outa here a minute ago, feller as wouldn't leave if the place was afire. Keep your eyes peeled when you leave."

The lawmen nodded gratefully, and he left them.

Massingham tried to lighten the

mood, "Can't see why Dorrell'd waste good money on gunnies for you, Brack." He chuckled and took a pull at his beer. "Why, any two-bit operator could put you under the ground!"

Brack returned the compliment, "Well, Mass, his money was easy come by! Would you believe that a certain sheriff damn near loaded it into his bag? He'da done that too, 'cept he was too busy feedin' his face!"

"Oh boy, did I ask for that one!" Massingham drawled as he sauntered to the counter for cigars.

Brack sat and listened to the whispers in the shadowed saloon. There were a few muttered greetings to a new arrival who didn't return them. Through the smoke-filled room the deputy watched the man carefully. Even from the back he looked like trouble.

Then the man turned round. His thin hair lay in lank strings on his forehead, and his face was grey and greasy. His black-clad frame was gaunt to the point of emaciation.

Dull green eyes flitted everywhere like crazed moths round a candle. Occasionally, they settled on the back of an unsuspecting drinker . . . A long knife was carried on his left thigh in a sheath, like a tied-down holster.

Brack bit his lip and frowned with distaste as the moth-like eyes settled on Massingham standing at the counter lighting a cigar. A gleam of recognition flared in them momentarily, and then they clouded over once more.

Brack's mind raced; this subhuman knew Massingham and probably had a score to settle. The signs were plain to read.

A taloned hand moved to the knife hilt. The man had moved to the other end of the counter. His right hand tapped it impatiently. He turned his head to whisper something before nodding towards the unsuspecting sheriff.

He and three other men moved at once. The speed of the movement was their undoing, as the three men deliberately shielded Phil Snare.

Massingham stubbed his cigar, reaching for an old tin that served as an ashtray. The barkeep whispered a warning, and he turned in a flash.

The three men had moved back. Snare's knife hand swept forward, the blade gleaming evilly as it started its arc up to the sheriff's stomach.

Brack rolled sideways off his stool. His Colt bellowed harshly in the confined space. No one moved or made a sound, except for Snare who screamed in agony. Nevertheless, the scarecrow of a man bent to pick up the knife right-handed.

Two more gunshots rocked the saloon, and Snare's screams climbed to a higher pitch. His left hand had already taken a bullet, leaving only a thumb hanging on a bloodied stump. Now the right hand danced like a puppet from a skein of sinew in a shower of blood.

As Massingham turned and vaulted the counter, blood spattered the men behind Snare. The axeman drew the axe from his belt. Another man shouted a warning.

It was too late.

The man who'd given it was watching Brack Bowman, and not Massingham. The Adams flew into the sheriff's hand and roared a message of death.

The .44 slug ricocheted off the axe blade and hit the man under his chin, bursting out under his ear. Cal the axeman was dead before his body thumped to the floor. Snare spared him no thought; he was howling like something demented as he knelt in a spreading puddle of his own blood.

The barkeep suddenly found his voice. "Damn you to hell, Phil Snare!" he screamed in a high, shocked tone. "Get outa here an' never show your face here again!"

Snare had lost too much blood to speak. Cursing his so-called friends soundlessly, he lurched to his feet and shuffled to the batwings. For a moment he teetered against them.

Then he collapsed outwards into the night.

* * *

Brack and Massingham rode away slowly.

At last the sheriff spoke. "Guess we're quits now, Brack. You saved my life. If you want, you can go back to Massingham Town and tell 'em what a mess I made." He cleared his throat. "An' I sure do thank you. My belly was 'bout a second from that knife. Cut it a bit fine, didn't you?"

Recalling Massingham's comment about the rattler, Brack grinned hugely. "Why Mass, that blade was a good half inch from your gut! Kinda jumpy ain't you?" Before the sheriff could reply, he added, "Ain't gonna tell no one 'bout you an' Roy handin' that money to Dorrell. Who'd believe me?"

Massingham pushed the pace to a gallop. For a while they were silent. Then he spoke reflectively. "Dunno what that guy had 'gainst me. Ain't never seen him."

Brack answered soberly, "Fellers like you 'n' me got more enemies than a wild dog has fleas." Then he chuckled, "Hey, some fast draw, Mass! How'd you get that bullet to go under that feller's chin 'n' come out o' his ear? You was taller'n him. Mighty tricky shootin'."

Massingham couldn't resist it. "Well, Brack my man, that there badge o' your'n is only a deputy's. When you're full sheriff, I'll teach you to get lucky like me!"

Ten miles into the night they bedded down. As they rolled into their tarps, the stars were cold points pricked through the black cloth of the night. Adrenalin was still pumping through their veins and sleep was elusive.

Massingham called wearily, "I was just thinkin' what an untidy cuss you are. All that blood; why didn't you shoot him nice 'n' clean, Brack?"

"Wasn't tryin' to kill him. Can't

stand knifemen. I just aimed to make sure he never used a knife again."

Massingham laughed mirthlessly, "You sure took care o' that, Mister Deputy."

Brack grunted in his tarp. "Didn't think 'bout tidiness when you killed that axeman. Blood comin' outta his ear like a volcano blowin' up. You an' your *full sheriff*'s shot!"

The sheriff yawned, "OK, I admit it. Aimed at his hand an' he got unlucky when the slug bounced off'n the axe . . . Careless shootin', I'm afraid."

"Speakin' 'personally," Brack began but was interrupted by a loud snore. Soon he too fell into dreamless sleep.

By ten o'clock the day was hot and sultry. As the lawmen cantered steadily in pursuit of their quarry, thunderheads built slowly ahead of them.

They pulled up in a small stand of pines to smoke and ease cramped muscles. Brack stared at the ground, a puzzled look in his eyes. He was stroking his beard gently, lost in thought.

The sheriff watched him awhile. Then he teased, "When you stand like that you look almost smart, Brack. You could make sheriff yet!"

Brack ignored the banter.

"Is that, or ain't that Old Forty's prints cuttin' 'cross that way?" he demanded.

Massingham came to take a look. "Sure's eggs're eggs. Them's his tracks. Let's follow 'em thataway. Reckon he just circled round a bit. Maybe Dorrell leathered his ass for stoppin'."

Still reluctant to ride, they followed the tracks on foot for nearly a mile. The sign showed clearly that the horse had passed that way not so long ago. Brack was of the opinion that since Dorrell had money, he might have run into somebody from whom he'd bought guns. If that had happened, he could be laying a trap, and caution was advisable.

Then they noticed that the trail had

looped round in a half circle leading back to Vengo.

"Might as well've sat an' waited right here," complained Massingham sourly, "Seems he's — " His words trailed off as they rounded a clump of sweet scented wild apples. A handsome chestnut was grazing placidly ahead.

Tension coiled their muscles like springs; they exchanged glances, and Brack inclined his head to indicate that they should approach from opposite directions.

Before they could move a voice rang out behind them. You're covered. Hands above your heads!"

The voice was high and shaky; it certainly wasn't Dorrell. Obediently they lifted their hands.

"Gonna backshoot us?" Massingham enquired, stalling for time. "Too scared t'show your face?"

"If'n I was gonna do that, I'da done it already," the youngster replied, "An' I ain't too scared to show my face."

He walked in front of them, his eyes

flicking over them. As he noted their stars, he holstered his guns.

"Oh shit, I'm real sorry, gents," he muttered, "But I already got held up once today."

Massingham looked over the dude cowboy gear and answered, "Where'd you get that hoss, young feller?"

"A guy got the drop on me. Crazy thing was, he changed hosses 'n' guns. He got my Winchester an' Colts, together with fifty dollars, the best o' the deal." He added bitterly, "Should've killed the bastard with his own guns. This blamed hoss won't go no further."

The lawmen surprised him by bursting into laughter.

Massingham gasped, "You'd as much chance o' pluggin' that jasper as you got o' movin' that hoss afore he's ready."

"I'm pretty quick on the draw, Sheriff," the boy said.

Brack intervened with a grim chuckle, "Listen son, ole Mass could give lessons to lightnin', but he couldn't kill no one, not with them guns o' your'n." Pointing at the horse, he added, "He'll only go when he's minded to. Right Mass?"

"Sure is. That's Ole Forty you got there. Goes like the wind for forty miles, then takes a long break."

The youngster looked crestfallen as he unshipped his guns. "Guess the shells from these only travel five feet, huh?"

"Try it an' see, son," urged the sheriff, his eyes twinkling.

The kid aimed at the chestnut, then thought better and drew a bead on a circling buzzard. The guns clicked uselessly.

Brack shook his head, "See why he changed 'em?"

The youngster's face was ashen, "He knew they wouldn't work? I sure was unlucky when I ran into him."

Massingham shook his head, "Unlucky? You musta been born under a *lucky* star. Wonder is he didn't shoot you right out. Musta tickled him exchangin' good guns for bad, an' a quirky hoss for a good one. Yours was a good one?"

"Yeah," the kid replied glumly, "I'm headed for Vengo when this hoss'll start."

"*Vengo?*" the lawmen cried in unison.

The boy blushed, "What's so surprisin' 'bout that? They tell me it's a great town," he finished suspiciously.

Brack tipped back his low-crowned Plainsman.

"You talk to loco'd cows? Who told you that?"

"My brother's ranch hands. It's full o' classy saloons, a real big casino with pretty gals, an' they got a Sheriff Goven — "

Massingham winked at Brack, "Don't recollect any Goven. How you spellin' that?"

The youngster looked exasperated as he spelled the name, "G.O.V.E.N., an' they got more gals than anywhere. Ain't a town like it in the world."

The lawmen looked at each other in silence. Brack stroked his beard and shook his head. Tapping his forehead,

Massingham muttered, "Touch o' the sun maybe."

The kid was getting riled, as well as suspicious.

"Go on then," he challenged, "You're bustin' your guts to tell me somethin' different, ain't you?"

Massingham fanned his face with his hat, then gazed at it thoughtfully. "If'n you're real lucky, you'd last 'bout an hour in Vengo. No law there. Rearrange the name Goven, and what do you get? Vengo! Folks there'd cut your throat for the price o' a beer. Yeah, I said cut your throat; bullets cost money! Them duds o' your'n would bring 'em outta their ratholes faster'n you could hitch your hoss."

A grim smile touched his lips, "Son, we just come from there. Killed two fellers, but there's plenty more waitin' for boys like you. Way we see it, even that jasper you met up with had to light out fast."

Brack weighed in, "Doubt if'n there's one gal in the whole damn town. In fact, a good-lookin' young feller like you could find himself entertainin' men friends."

"My stepbrother's behind this," the youngster whispered through bloodless lips. "He allus wanted the ranch. I'll kill the bastard for this."

"Not with them guns," Brack said.

He slipped from his saddle and dug round in the spare horse's saddle-bags. "Here kid, this ole Navy Colt's a .36. Ain't fancy, but I plugged five owlhoots with it. Can't have you ridin' round with useless guns, now can we?"

The youngster took the weapon gratefully. "Sure am obliged to you. Hell, what a fool I've been."

Brack handed over a box of shells. "What's your name, son?"

"John Grantley, sir. Stepbrother is Wil Grantley. We own the Double Circle G."

"Well, John, I'm Deputy Bowman from Lewis. This here's Sheriff Massingham, from the town o' that name."

182

"*The* Sheriff Massingham? You got a mighty fine town — "

Brack laughed heartily, Yeah, you oughta try visitin' *his* town if'n you're keen on travellin'. Give Vengo a miss."

"Vengo? Never heard o' it!"

Massingham chipped in, "What sorta hoss did you trade with that jasper, young feller?"

"Grey mare. You can track her easy. Both back shoes are worn bad. I was going to get 'em fixed in Vengo."

Brack's reply was spine-chilling, "If'n you'd gone to Vengo you'd be lyin' dead in the street. No bone yards. Your hoss would be fillin' the bellies o' half the town. Take my advice an' ride to Massingham Town or Lewis. I gotta twin brother Wes, runs the casino there. He'll look after you, an' he's got some real pretty gals. An' see the sheriff," he finished gruffly, "Tell him I ain't run away from him, huh?"

13

BY now Dorrell would have increased his lead and the lawmen were reluctant to rest. As young Grantley had predicted, they found no difficulty in picking up his grey mare's tracks, and they pushed on until dusk was thick around them.

Nevertheless, the danger of injuring a horse in a pothole in the dark in an area where shale and holes abounded was too great. Once more they were forced to stop for the night.

Wrapped in their tarps they tried hard to sleep, but the more they tried the more sleep eluded them. Massingham's worry was that if too much time passed, news of the foul-up at the bank might leak out. He didn't blame Roy; his old friend had been ill and under the doctor's medicine. He should never have been subject to the task Massingham had laid upon him.

Another fear hounded him. Suppose Dorrell met someone who stole the money from him. In a dumb-ox way Dorrell was tough but he'd be no match for a fast gunman. A gang might split the money and scatter just about anywhere. If that happened, he could go waltzing all over the country.

Brack's thoughts were as bleak. He'd left Wes, his mother and sister, to chase Dorrell. Lewis was a thriving town with a circuit judge who was Brack's father-in-law. It was unfortunate that he'd had to leave so soon after his appointment as deputy. Wes would leave his night-club casino 'Night Birds' in the hands of trusted staff and help the sheriff, but who could guess what might happen? As if driven by some malevolent force outside himself, his mind turned to his dead wife Rachel. She and their baby had only been dead a few weeks, and the loss of them had followed the death of a first wife.

His whole life had been studded with

disaster. He had to avenge his father by killing Dorrell, and go back to Lewis. Return to what? No golden-haired, green-eyed Rachel, that was for sure.

He sat up in his tarp and hunted his Bull Durham. Soon he'd found it and was smoking morosely. In the moonlight he saw Massingham rolling restlessly, as sleepless as himself. What a pair, he thought bitterly.

The air was thick and warm, unnaturally so for this early hour. He heard a distant rumble and saw lightning stutter over the horizon. Somewhere someone was getting a storm. Well, let 'em keep it, he thought bleakly. If'n it breaks round here it'll be Mass 'n' me gettin' drowned. Like as not, with our luck, we'll get hit by lightnin'.

Before the sun was up they were back on the trail, acutely aware of the ever denser atmosphere. The thunder came more loudly and frequently, and sometimes lightning forked right up across the sky.

The country was broken with small hills and outcrops with occasional blasted trees twisting stark, blackened arms in bleak supplication. A brooding silence gripped the land. In the yellowing sky buzzards soared, their wings spread and black, seeking death. The mountains towered ahead in shifting shades of purple, blue, violet, and sometimes black.

Through a pair of field glasses they took turns scanning the way ahead, never forgetting that Dorrell now had John's Winchester to replace the Hawken he'd left at the gatehouse. The rumpled land kept their quarry from view, and their nerves stretched steadily tighter.

"Can't be more'n four hours ahead," growled Brack at length. "What d'you reckon?"

Massingham mopped his brow with a bandanna that was dark with sweat. "Guess you're 'bout right. We oughta catch up just before the mountains."

"Reckon he's spotted us?"

"How in hell can I tell?" Massingham replied irritably. "Since we ain't seen a hair o' him, likely he ain't seen us. Thanks to John, he's got a coupla .45s an' a Winchester, so stay awake."

Now storm clouds were massing ahead. A hot breeze buffeted their faces as they entered a forbiddingly dark canyon. Behind a large rockfall they pulled in to brew coffee and fry ham and beans.

As they finished the light midday meal, the wind picked up to bellow down the canyon and fling dust into their faces. Fir trees that had rustled with wind and lurched drunkenly when they entered the canyon now swayed like giant pendulums. At the far end on level ground two caves gaped at them like the sockets in a skull.

"In there!" shouted Brack and they vaulted into their saddles. As they galloped for the caves, rain slashed down in stinging torrents that blinded them in seconds.

As suddenly as it had started,

the rain stopped. The air prickled with the acrid smell of ozone as once more sand blasted down the canyon. The screaming wind whipped it into a frenzied whirl that drove it straight through the bandannas wrapped round their faces. Soon an enormous mushroom cloud blotted out the sky and the air turned a dark smoky brown. Suddenly lightning zigzagged into rocks a few yards to the left and an ear-splitting clap of thunder exploded over them.

Still they hadn't reached the caves, and they raked their spurs down the horses' sides for a final dash. At last, pursued by howling demons of wind, they made the refuge, and slid from their saddles. Hobbling their mounts in one cave, they grabbed their gear and pelted through the storm to the other.

No sooner were they inside it than ball lightning rolled in eerie blue light along the canyon floor. Trees, scrub and rocks flickered in outlines of black in the ghastly light. Knowing what could have happened to them if they'd been caught outside, they looked at each other and grinned wanly.

Massingham voiced the thought in both their minds, "Hope that bastard Dorrell's enjoyin' this."

Brack's face was stony. "Just so long's it don't kill him afore I get to him."

The sheriff didn't push it; they both had an interest in seeing that Dorrell came back dead.

Suddenly the storm was over. The lightning spluttered into silence and the sky turned a dirty sulphur colour. With sighs of relief, the lawmen got their horses from the other cave and moved off.

Massingham led, gigging his buckskin up a small incline for a view through the field glasses. Brack followed, trying to light a cigar in the breeze that still whipped around him.

Massingham called back, "Hey Brack, shift your ass up here. Maybe your eyes are better'n mine. Can't see that grey out there."

Brack grunted and pushed his mount up to Massingham.

It was then that the storm played its final card.

Suddenly everything stood out in sharp relief as blue light washed the land. From a dark green sky a thunderbolt crashed into a petrified stump not far off, instantly reducing it to smouldering dust.

With a terrified scream, the sheriff's horse rose to its hind legs, throwing its luckless rider like a cork from a bottle. As his head cracked sickly on the ground it seemed that the storm was raging anew in his brain.

He lurched to his feet, and would have fallen if Brack hadn't been out of his saddle and ready to catch him.

"You ain't goin' nowhere for a while, Mass," he growled. "Sit a bit; Dorrell can keep awhile."

Massingham was in no shape to argue.

"Thanks Brack," he gasped, "I know what this means to you. Go on alone." He poured water from his canteen over his head and grinned weakly, "An' don't go ridin' off with that money, eh?"

Brack smiled bleakly. "I'll wait; ain't goin' on without you."

He flicked a match on a thumbnail and lit a cigar.

"Here Mass; it'll make a new man o' you."

Massingham took it gratefully. While he smoked, Brack picked up the field glasses and studied the way ahead. The blue-grey cones of the mountains seemed to loom a mere short walk away, but nothing moved except drifting buzzards.

Massingham drew hard on his cigar. "Probably just crawlin' outa cover, like us. If'n the wind drops, with this sun, we ain't gonna see nothin' but steam."

Steam was already wreathing the ground, and Brack snorted angrily.

"Shit Mass, everythin's against us an' workin' for that sonofabitch!"

Massingham agreed ruefully. "Looks that way. First the goddamn river's swelled by rain. Then somethin' scares him outa Vengo ahead o' us, that kid gives him a handgun, a Winchester an' a hoss. Now I fall off'n my own hoss 'n' knock out what little brains I had."

"Mass, I'd say you got a shove. That thunderbolt did spook your hoss a mite."

Massingham gazed at the smouldering remains of the petrified stump. "Yeah, I reckon if'n your beard had caught fire you'da been a mite spooked."

Brack paled. "Hell's teeth! I was right next to there when you called me to shift my ass!"

Massingham was still rubbing his head; he grinned at his companion, "Don't know how you got through your days without me, an' I reckon you've used up your luck as it is. What with rattlers, axemen an' lightnin', you must be near as lucky as Dorrell!"

Dorrell was indeed feeling lucky. He'd found a crack in the canyon wall wide enough for the grey and himself. Overhead the crack petered out to form a natural roof so that he'd sheltered in what was virtually a small cave.

When he'd moved into the cave the storm hadn't been too bad; then it had returned to rake the canyon with greater severity. Looking back, he'd thanked his lucky stars. Yes, fate was good to him.

Now he was at the river which skirted the foothills. He jigged the horse slowly to the water's edge. Normally, the river was deep and sluggish; now it was a swirling maelstrom, fed by hundreds of rivulets from the mountains.

Soon a stocky, tough looking cowhand joined him, working his way along the river. The man rode a huge old piebald. His freckled face and arms were burned near black from countless hours in the saddle and tufts of hair sprouted from his nose and ears. A battered grey hat was pushed to the back of his head and in one hand he carried a shotgun.

"Easy as spittin'," he rasped. "When you know the right place."

Dorrell tried on a smile. "Maybe for an experienced feller like you. Us city folk ain't so clever in situations like this."

The other man nodded. "Reckon so, mister. Just you follow me an' see how it's done." He walked his horse a little way along to where the river narrowed.

Dorrell shook his head dubiously. "Damn river looks faster here."

The man leaned sideways and spat a near black stream of tobacco juice. "It's shallower." He pointed with a calloused finger, "See that ole tree wedged 'tween the bank an' that there rock?"

"Yeah," Dorrell grated, irked by the man's contempt for him as a city slicker, "I ain't aimin' to jump there. Hoss ain't born as can do that."

The cowhand spat again, then jerked a lariat from his saddle-horn and swung it round his head. As the rope whistled across the water and dropped over a branch projecting from the tree, he grunted, "I'm from Texas, just north o' the Rio Grande." With a flick of his wrist the noose was tightened.

Dorrell muttered grudgingly, "So the ole sayin's true?"

The cowhand grinned, exposing discoloured teeth. "Yeah, Texans can throw a rope with their feet better'n a Mex can with his hands."

Dorrell folded his arms and shook his head. "OK so far, but now we gotta pull the goddam tree back 'cross that current, then get the hosses to paddle us, huh?"

The cowhand rubbed a bristly jaw. "Nope," he drawled. "If'n them hosses dropped the paddle, we'd be like to get wet! No, we snub this end to the bank; then we swim our hosses across, holdin' on the rope. I mean *we* hold on, got it?"

Dorrell's mouth thinned; this guy was getting to him, and no mistake. "Ain't nothin' to tie up to, far's I can see," he growled.

The other man slipped from his horse. From a saddle-bag he produced a loop of hard steel with an eye at one end. Rummaging in the bag, he found another straight piece, lashed the two together with rawhide and hammered the metal into the ground with a rock until only the eye showed.

"There y'are city boy. Magic ain't it? Ain't it just amazin' what us simple cowhands can do?"

Dorrell's nostrils flared. "Gonna show this dumb city slicker how to cross? If'n you do, I'll see you get a proper reward."

"Sure, no trouble." The man pointed again. "One more reason for crossin' here. See them prickly pears? A trail starts there, leads right to the top o' that mountain. See that ledge up there, near a mile away. Your eyes good 'nough?"

You stinkin' Texan, Dorrell thought savagely, you'll see who's the smart one soon enough.

The cowhand rode his piebald to the water's edge, spat at the torrent, then forked his mount into the foaming water. Within seconds he was swimming the animal, the rope gripped in his big fists as he stood in his stirrups.

Halfway across the river, he bellowed over the roar of the water, "Hey city boy, easy ain't it?"

"Easy as pluggin' a smartass!" Dorrell screamed as he levelled the Winchester.

The cowhand's grin froze as he looked back at death.

Before he could speak Dorrell's first bullet shattered his neck, two more passed through his lungs and heart, and a third caught him at the base of his spine as he slid over his horse's neck. His body disappeared into the water and was swept downstream.

Dorrell took a small telescope from his pocket and put it to his eye. He stared up at the ledge a mile away below the mountain top. "Well, grey mare," he chuckled, "We gotta swim. Leastways *you* have to."

The mare snorted and backed off but Dorrell dug his spur hard in her sides. Soon horse and rider arrived dripping and panting on the other bank.

Dorrell looked back at the water complacently, then cut the rope. He'd climb to the ledge, rest up awhile, and easily be able to spot any pursuers. He noted that the water was still rising. If Sheriff Massingham was after him, he'd need to fly. Once he reached the mountain-top he'd be clear; free to go straight to Mexico. A long ride, but the gods had been with him so far, and nothing could stop him now.

He lifted his arms to the sky and shouted in triumph, "Frankie Dorrell's the tops!"

Then an icy wind whistled down the mountainside and plucked the new hat he'd chosen in Massingham Town from his head. With gloomy foreboding he watched it skim the surface of the brown waters. It passed the piebald which by then had almost drowned on the end of the severed rope and sank into the river.

As a shiver racked Dorrell's frame, rain fell in chill torrents . . .

14

BY nightfall the lawmen reached the foot of the mountain range and followed the tracks to the exact spot where Dorrell had crossed. The raging torrent of the river was impassable, the gale force winds whipping the waters into vicious white teeth.

Massingham and Brack Bowman gazed at the frenzied river with renewed gloom.

However, Frankie Dorrell was also far from happy.

For a start, the path up the mountains was a lot steeper than he'd expected. But that wasn't all; water pouring down the path in miniature rivers made the footing slippery and treacherous, and the freezing wind gusted and snatched at him, threatening to hurl him over the edge at any moment.

Long before he reached the ledge near the top, he was forced to stop. Tethering his horse to a stunted pine, he squeezed into a large crevice. It was poor shelter; water cascaded onto him and his body was racked with shivers throughout the night. By daybreak, he ached everywhere.

Nevertheless, before the night ended, the rain and wind abruptly stopped. The water on the path slowed to a trickle as the moon, rind-thin and grey as a corpse, lit the way. Dorrell pushed slowly on, his one thought to get higher, reach the ledge and make coffee which he could lace with whisky. Then he'd get on to the summit, and freedom.

The going was still slippery, the light poor, and the grey was reluctant. Forced to lead the way, Dorrell muttered angrily. Once the terrified animal stopped suddenly so that Dorrell lost his footing and slithered towards it on his back. Fortunately, he managed to keep his hold on the reins, but he cursed long and fluently.

At last, every muscle complaining at the violent exercise, the cold and damp, he reached the ledge. Hobbling the horse, he flung himself down on his back and waited for daylight.

When the sun pushed up in a red line on the horizon, the land was bathed in a coppery glow. The sky took on the depth and blueness which presaged a hot day, and buzzards wheeled and drifted on rising air currents. With his telescope, Dorrell followed them to where the river narrowed downstream.

Ancient oak trees gripped the banks and the river-bed with tenacious roots. Dorrell adjusted his glass. There it was, the body of the cowhand, and a little further down were the remains of his horse. The carrion birds were already at work on them.

Dorrell's mouth twisted in a grin, "Big-headed Texans, you never know when to keep your traps shut!"

Idly he swept the telescope a little

way upstream from his vantage point. What he saw wiped the grin from his face.

Poking at a fire was that scar-faced sonofabitching sheriff, and he guessed that was a deputy sitting up in a tarp drinking coffee. Although it was a mile distant his glass showed the steam curling over the cup.

He studied the man with the coffee and his grip tightened on the telescope. As recognition dawned on him, cold fingers walked up his spine. Brack Bowman! The bastard had joined up with Massingham, and now they were both on his trail.

However, the river was still high and fast; in places it had overflowed its banks, and he'd got a Winchester and the element of surprise. He was going to end it right there.

Approaching the grey carefully (he didn't want any bucking and rearing, and the horse was scared of him), he drew the gun from the saddle scabbard. The weapon was shining new and felt good in his hands, well balanced and smelling of oil. The 1873 .44 was the cowhand model, a good rifle but without a long range, though Dorrell (who was no expert on weapons) didn't know that.

He chuckled grimly, "What a nice mornin' for asshole shootin'! It's like they're just a half mile off."

For a moment he pondered who to kill first. Not that it mattered a damn; in a couple of seconds he'd take care of them both. His hands shook and were damp on the stock of the gun, and his breathing quickened and whistled with excitement.

★ ★ ★

Both lawmen were tense and irritable after their cold, wet night and, when the sun had come up it had shown them that the river was faster and wider than before. In places it had spread out over the land and, for the time being at least, crossing was impossible. They'd built up a fire and were drying out and eating breakfast.

Now Massingham walked over to Brack to hand him a couple of biscuits. He stood, lighting a cigar, and gazed moodily across the water. Scanning the mountainside, he saw the grey mare, and the glint of sunlight on metal.

"He's up there, Brack. Under cover!"

"What cover?" Brack retorted as he rolled from his tarp.

Realizing that he was as exposed on his ledge as the lawmen on the bank, Dorrell snapped off a shot at Massingham. Buzzards circled lazily upwards at the bark of the Winchester.

Massingham and Brack looked at each other and grinned as they heard a plop from the river.

"He's either a rotten shot or he's outa range," Brack grunted.

Again the Winchester barked, and once more the water plopped. Nevertheless, the lawmen found what cover they could.

"Fish are bitin' well this mornin'," Brack shouted from behind a log.

Only partly covered by a small rock, Massingham grinned hugely. "Hey Brack! I gotta great idea. Why — "

Brack cut across him, "Trouble is, Mass, some o' your ideas are apt to go wrong."

Massingham ignored this. "Listen, he's outa range. When he shoots, let's play possum. Let him think we're dead. Then we pop up — "

Brack called back wearily, "Mass — "

"No, listen. We'll stand close together. That way he ain't gonna know who he's plugged. He'll get slack."

Brack considered a moment. "OK, let's do it."

They stood together and peered up at where Dorrell lay cursing his rifle, unaware that the distance was too great for it.

Then Dorrell saw that they'd moved together.

"Stupid bastards, standin' there like that," he exulted. "Can't miss 'em."

"You can die first, Brack," the sheriff muttered.

"Thanks, it's a priv — " Brack began.

Once more the Winchester barked.

Dorrell's heart leapt as he saw Brack Bowman crumple to the ground.

"Sheriff, you got lucky," he chortled. "That was meant for *you*." As he watched Massingham bend over the 'dead' Bowman, he giggled crazily. "Bye bye Sheriff, I got the hang o' this gun now."

Another shot and the sheriff was on his knees, then collapsing onto the deputy from Lewis. Dorrell capered in glee.

Down by the river Brack was laughing at Massingham.

"Hell Mass, if'n you don't get off'n me soon, we'll haveta get hitched!"

"My mom told me never to marry a bearded man, specially a poor deputy. Keep still a minute!" Massingham retorted.

On the ledge Dorrell's joy knew no

bounds. The night had been cold and wet, and he'd been badly frightened by seeing Bowman and Massingham together. Now they were both off his back. He'd got a stack of money from the bank, a new horse and guns, and freedom was his. Everything was smelling of roses.

Holding up the rifle, he danced towards his horse.

"How's that for shootin', grey mare? Better'n your dude any day!"

The grey shook her head and snorted violently. Dorrell unhobbled her, his state of euphoria sweeping away his aches and pains. His brain clicked along at top speed, working out plans.

"Come on, hoss, ain't stoppin' for nothin'. Over this mountain, and we're in heaven."

Just to make sure, he used the telescope to check the dead lawmen a last time. No mistake about it; they were as stiff as that big-mouthed Texan. Fumbling the telescope back into his pocket, he dropped the reins and then the telescope itself. Cursing, he jumped after it as it rolled towards the edge.

At once his luck changed. As he scrabbled round for the telescope, his horse backed nervously away. Tossing her head, she whickered loudly, and Massingham's buckskin down below answered with a shrill whistle.

That was all it took. The grey mare wheeled and trotted straight back down the path, taking Dorrell's dreams of wealth with her. Speechless with rage, his eyes bulging, he watched his money return to the water's edge far below.

Cautiously, Massingham lifted his head, looked across the river, and grinned broadly as he saw the horse coming down the path.

"Look, that's my money coming back," he told Brack triumphantly.

Brack grunted beneath him, "Bet you wish you could whistle up gals like that. Now all you gotta do's get across an' collect it without gettin' shot. You can bet Dorrell'll be comin' right after it."

"Hop up an' dance a jig to catch his attention. Then I can plug him in the leg."

Brack answered sarcastically, "Can't dance, no music! An' how you gonna get him? Ain't you noticed the range is the same each way?"

"Well, we can lay here till he comes for the money an' then — "

Brack reacted instantly. "No! He could be more'n an hour, an' I ain't sure it's your Adams stickin' up my ass!"

Massingham grinned devilishly. "*You* can't reach him; *your* rifle won't send a slug no further than his. But I got my ole Hawken, good for a full mile, Mister Deputy."

"I bet Mr Dorrell wishes he hadn't left the one he stole from that trapper at the gatehouse. If'n he hadn't done, we'd be dead for real by now."

He squirmed out from under the sheriff.

"He ain't goin' nowhere; ain't 'nough to hide a lizard up there."

On the ledge Dorrell was foaming at the mouth as he hurled obscenities after the grey mare. Then he paused to apply the telescope to his eye.

Down on the river-bank both lawmen were on their feet.

Massingham was drawing his rifle from his saddle-boot, and understanding burst upon Dorrell. He'd been out of range all the time, and fear twisted his gut with cold fingers. Then, his hands sweating on the telescope, he felt his mood gyrate. If he hadn't been able to reach them, they couldn't get to him.

Jubilantly, he stalked up and down the ledge and hurled abuse at them. Then a thought struck him; why not shoot the damn grey as it stood looking across the river? Crazed by bloodlust, he quite forgot that he'd need the beast to carry his money.

Massingham shook his head in disgust as he looked at the .60 Hawken in his hands. "Shit, this ain't mine!! Tom mixed mine up with the trapper's."

Brack regarded him stonily. "One

Hawken's same as another."

Massingham flushed. "How do I know this one's set up? I don't want to kill him, just wing him. The notches on this gun're for buffalo, I reckon — "

He broke off, his jaw hanging.

Brack's Colt was levelled at his chest. His eyes bored unwaveringly into Massingham.

"Real sorry, Sheriff," he drawled, "I'll take that gun. If'n you please."

Massingham gulped. He couldn't believe this was happening. "Hey Brack, it's my town's money he took!"

Brack pointed up at the ledge with his free hand his smile wolfish, Your money, Mass, but my pa's killer's up there."

At that moment Dorrell's Winchester barked, and the grey mare sank to her knees. As the lawmen watched, she collapsed onto her side, and blood washed out of her mouth.

Brack's Colt remained unwavering.

Massingham recalled his own hunt for the killers of his parents. He nodded his understanding to Brack.

"OK Brack, put your iron away. You wouldn't gun me down any more'n I'd shoot you; we're on the same side, remember?"

Brack's face reflected a range of conflicting emotions. Then he leathered his weapon.

"Thanks Mass," he breathed. You know how it is. Smart lawyers can do terrible things. That sonofabitch up there murdered my pa an' a lotta other people. Now he's killed that hoss outa spite. He ain't fit to live."

Handing him the Hawken, Massingham observed drily, "Gonna miss first time, but he ain't got no cover. You'll get him 'fore he reaches the top; you gotta whole box o' shells!!"

★ ★ ★

Dorrell teetered on the edge, unhinged by the turn of events. He was safe enough; the range was too great for — Then his thoughts crashed together

214

as fragments of conversation echoed in his brain. Was it Massingham speaking? The old trapper? It was the old gatehouse man. "Nice ole rifle . . . The sheriff's got one like it . . . Kill a buffalo at a mile . . . at a mile . . . "

His body sheathed in sweat, he looked through the telescope. Bowman was the one taking a bead on him, and he let out a long, shaky breath. Surely the lawmen couldn't both have Hawkens?

Then fear rushed at him again. Bowman's shot would fall short. Then Massingham would open up with his Hawken, and there wasn't any cover . . .

* * *

Massingham bent over.

"Here's your chance to kick my ass," he laughed, "But if'n you want some support, you can lay the Hawken 'cross my back. It's a bitch o' a recoil, maybe

215

too much for a deputy!"

Grimly Brack nodded his gratitude, and knelt to ensure the best possible shot. Laying the gun across Massingham's back, he took a deep, slow breath. Banishing the thoughts of what Dorrell had done to his family, he caressed the trigger as he sighted on his enemy.

Squeeze a little more, a shade more, pause, gently, so gently . . .

The roar of the Hawken nearly deafened both lawmen. His ears ringing, Massingham stood and looked through the field glasses.

The effect on a human head of being struck by a slug from the Hawken was equivalent to that of being hit at ten yards by a small cannonball. Dorrell's head had ceased to exist. The soft-nosed bullet favoured by the old trapper had spread on impact, and blood and brains spattered the ground around the corpse.

"Well?" demanded Brack. "Did I get him?"

Massingham wiped the field glasses

on the sleeve of his shirt. He made a show of peering through them again.

"'Fraid you were a mite high," he drawled.

"How much is a mite?"

"Well." Massingham looked through the glasses again. "If'n you was aimin' to wing him it was a poor shot, but I reckon he ain't gonna wear no more hats!"

Brack's voice tremored. "It's all over then. You can pick up your money soon's we can cross the river."

The sheriff handed across his hip-flask. "Time to celebrate. Strange how fate works, ain't it?"

Brack took a pull at the flask. "How's that, Mass?"

"Dorrell killed that trapper an' took his gun. That gun made me suspect him straight off. Then he met young John, an' swopped ole Forty for his grey."

He mopped his face with his bandanna, "Now that worn't good luck for him 'cos when my hoss called, his'n came trottin' right down."

Brack handed back the flask. "Guess you're right at that. I shot him with the gun he'd stolen, purely 'cos your ole Tom mixed 'em up!"

Massingham slapped him on the back. "Worn't too bad a shot for a deputy!"

Brack slipped his army knife from its sheath and examined the stock of the Hawken. He muttered under his breath as he whetted the blade, "Not much room."

Puzzled by his behaviour, Massingham leaned over to see what he was doing.

"What you doin' Brack?"

Brack didn't answer at once. He found a spot on the stock of the gun, and applied the blade deftly.

Then he looked up with a grim smile. "Just puttin' the *final* notch on it. Kinda rounds things off nicely, don't it?"

Massingham gazed thoughtfully across the river. He lit a cigar and blew grey smoke into the hot sunshine.

Yeah," he replied drily. "Guess you could say that. Or you could say it was one from the grave . . . Now, let's see if'n I can get that money without gettin' drowned."

THE END

Other titles in the
Linford Western Library:

TOP HAND
Wade Everett

The Broken T was big. But no ranch is big enough to let a man hide from himself.

GUN WOLVES OF LOBO BASIN
Lee Floren

The Feud was a blood debt. When Smoke Talbot found the outlaws who gunned down his folks he aimed to nail their hide to the barn door.

SHOTGUN SHARKEY
Marshall Grover

The westbound coach carrying the indomitable Larry and Stretch headed for a shooting showdown.

FIGHTING RAMROD
Charles N. Heckelmann

Most men would have cut their losses, but Frazer counted the bullets in his guns and said he'd soak the range in blood before he'd give up another inch of what was his.

LONE GUN
Eric Allen

Smoke Blackbird had been away too long. The Lequires had seized the Blackbird farm, forcing the Indians and settlers off, and no one seemed willing to fight! He had to fight alone.

THE THIRD RIDER
Barry Cord

Mel Rawlins wasn't going to let anything stand in his way. His father was murdered, his two brothers gone. Now Mel rode for vengeance.

ARIZONA DRIFTERS
W. C. Tuttle

When drifting Dutton and Lonnie Steelman decide to become partners they find that they have a common enemy in the formidable Thurston brothers.

TOMBSTONE
Matt Braun

Wells Fargo paid Luke Starbuck to outgun the silver-thieving stagecoach gang at Tombstone. Before long Luke can see the only thing bearing fruit in this eldorado will be the gallows tree.

HIGH BORDER RIDERS
Lee Floren

Buckshot McKee and Tortilla Joe cut the trail of a border tough who was running Mexican beef into Texas. They stopped the smuggler in his tracks.

BRETT RANDALL, GAMBLER
E. B. Mann

Larry Day had the choice of running away from the law or of assuming a dead man's place. No matter what he decided he was bound to end up dead.

THE GUNSHARP
William R. Cox

The Eggerleys weren't very smart. They trained their sights on Will Carney and Arizona's biggest blood bath began.

THE DEPUTY OF SAN RIANO
Lawrence A. Keating and
Al. P. Nelson

When a man fell dead from his horse, Ed Grant was spotted riding away from the scene. The deputy sheriff rode out after him and came up against everything from gunfire to dynamite.

FARGO: MASSACRE RIVER
John Benteen

The ambushers up ahead had now blocked the road. Fargo's convoy was a jumble, a perfect target for the insurgents' weapons!

SUNDANCE: DEATH IN THE LAVA
John Benteen

The Modoc's captured the wagon train and its cargo of gold. But now the halfbreed they called Sundance was going after it . . .

HARSH RECKONING
Phil Ketchum

Five years of keeping himself alive in a brutal prison had made Brand tough and careless about who he gunned down . . .

FARGO: PANAMA GOLD
John Benteen

With foreign money behind him, Buckner was going to destroy the Panama Canal before it could be completed. Fargo's job was to stop Buckner.

FARGO: THE SHARPSHOOTERS
John Benteen

The Canfield clan, thirty strong were raising hell in Texas. Fargo was tough enough to hold his own against the whole clan.

PISTOL LAW
Paul Evan Lehman

Lance Jones came back to Mustang for just one thing — revenge! Revenge on the people who had him thrown in jail.

HELL RIDERS
Steve Mensing

Wade Walker's kid brother, Duane, was locked up in the Silver City jail facing a rope at dawn. Wade was a ruthless outlaw, but he was smart, and he had vowed to have his brother out of jail before morning!

DESERT OF THE DAMNED
Nelson Nye

The law was after him for the murder of a marshal — a murder he didn't commit. Breen was after him for revenge — and Breen wouldn't stop at anything . . . blackmail, a frameup . . . or murder.

DAY OF THE COMANCHEROS
Steven C. Lawrence

Their very name struck terror into men's hearts — the Comancheros, a savage army of cutthroats who swept across Texas, leaving behind a bloodstained trail of robbery and murder.

SUNDANCE: SILENT ENEMY
John Benteen

A lone crazed Cheyenne was on a personal war path. They needed to pit one man against one crazed Indian. That man was Sundance.

LASSITER
Jack Slade

Lassiter wasn't the kind of man to listen to reason. Cross him once and he'll hold a grudge for years to come — if he let you live that long.

LAST STAGE TO GOMORRAH
Barry Cord

Jeff Carter, tough ex-riverboat gambler, now had himself a horse ranch that kept him free from gunfights and card games. Until Sturvesant of Wells Fargo showed up.

McALLISTER
ON THE
COMANCHE CROSSING
Matt Chisholm

The Comanche, McAllister owes them a life — and the trail is soaked with the blood of the men who had tried to outrun them before.

QUICK-TRIGGER COUNTRY
Clem Colt

Turkey Red hooked up with Curly Bill Graham's outlaw crew. But wholesale murder was out of Turk's line, so when range war flared he bucked the whole border gang alone . . . .

CAMPAIGNING
Jim Miller

Ambushed on the Santa Fe trail, Sean Callahan is saved by two Indian strangers. But there'll be more lead and arrows flying before the band join Kit Carson against the Comanches.

GUNSLINGER'S RANGE
Jackson Cole

Three escaped convicts are out for revenge. They won't rest until they put a bullet through the head of the dirty snake who locked them behind bars.

RUSTLER'S TRAIL
Lee Floren

Jim Carlin knew he would have to stand up and fight because he had staked his claim right in the middle of Big Ike Outland's best grass.

THE TRUTH ABOUT SNAKE RIDGE
Marshall Grover

The troubleshooters came to San Cristobal to help the needy. For Larry and Stretch the turmoil began with a brawl and then an ambush.

WOLF DOG RANGE
Lee Floren

Will Ardery would stop at nothing, unless something stopped him first — like a bullet from Pete Manly's gun.

DEVIL'S DINERO
Marshall Grover

Plagued by remorse, a rich old reprobate hired the Texas Trouble-shooters to deliver a fortune in greenbacks to each of his victims.

GUNS OF FURY
Ernest Haycox

Dane Starr, alias Dan Smith, wanted to close the door on his past and hang up his guns, but people wouldn't let him.

DONOVAN
Elmer Kelton

Donovan was supposed to be dead. Uncle Joe Vickers had fired off both barrels of a shotgun into the vicious outlaw's face as he was escaping from jail. Now Uncle Joe had been shot — in just the same way.

CODE OF THE GUN
Gordon D. Shirreffs

MacLean came riding home, with saddle tramp written all over him, but sewn in his shirt-lining was an Arizona Ranger's star.

GAMBLER'S GUN LUCK
Brett Austen

Gamblers seldom live long. Parker was a hell of a gambler. It was his life — or his death . . .

1	2/04	25		49		73		
2		26		50	4/19	74		
3		27		51		75		
4	7/02	28		52		76		
5		29		53		77		
6		30		54		78		
7		31		55		79	12/01	
8	6/24	32		56		80		
9	4/2	33		57	7/11	81		
10	.	34		58		82		
11		35		59		83		
12	4/05	36		60		84		
13		37		61	5/23 6/10	85		
14		38		62		86		
15	7/05	39	12/21	63		87		
16		40		64		88		
17		41		65		89		
18		42		66		90		
19		43		67		91		
20		44	12/22	68		92		
21	12/11 2/24	45		69		COMMUNITY SERVICES		
22		46		70				
23		47		71		NPT/111		
24		48		72		.		